GECKO MAGIC

THE ELEMENTAL KEYS BOOK 3

LYNNE CANTWELL

hearth/myth

Table of Contents

How We Got Here 1

Chapter 1 – Friday, in transit 3

Chapter 2 – the forever Friday 11

Chapter 3 – Saturday with a smoking volcanic pit 20

Chapter 4 – still Saturday, but with home cooking 29

Chapter 5 – Sunday with little men 40

Chapter 6 – Sunday with Auntie Helen and friends 52

Chapter 7 – still Sunday, now with aumakua 58

Chapter 8 – still Sunday 68

Chapter 9 – just your typical Monday 78

Chapter 10 – Monday, down where it's wetter 88

Chapter 11 – nowhere, doing very little 96

Chapter 12 – the longest Monday in the history of ever, but then Tuesday
.... 105

Chapter 13 – Tuesday, on a Rocky Mountain high 112

Chapter 14 – an easy Tuesday drive (as if) 122

Chapter 15 – possibly the longest two-hour drive in history 130

Chapter 16 – how to cage your demon 141

Author's Note 145

About the Author 147

HOW WE GOT HERE

So here we are again, the four of us, getting on a plane and chasing our tails. How does this keep happening?

Let's recap: The stars of our story are four half-human Elementals: Gail Oleander, the Airy half-sylph; Rufus McKay, the Fiery half-salamander (the magic kind, not the lives-under-your-porch kind); Collum Barth, the Earthy half-gnome; and me, Raney Meadows, a Watery half-undine and out-of-work actress. We met in Harpers Ferry, West Virginia, where the spirit of the Shenandoah River put Collum's brother's dead body where I would find it. Then Collum found me, we met the others, a guy named Cassius swept us away to a crucible where we exchanged Elemental juices, and hey presto, we were a team – although not the well-oiled machine we ought to be, considering we all have a part of each other within us now.

We even have superhero names. I'm the Torrent. We still don't have a team name, though. Or spandex costumes. Or even t-shirts. I am really put out about not having t-shirts. I mean, if we were a bocce ball team, we'd have t-shirts.

Maybe we need a corporate sponsor.

Anyway, Collum's brother Conor was killed because he knew too much. See, my father, Damien Jones – who's a narcissistic sociopath, among his other endearing traits – had played a long con on a guy who owned a construction company in West Virginia. Damien, or rather the ancient evil thing riding him, made the guy a state representative in exchange for helping him lop off the top of a mountain to get to a big coal seam underneath. Unfortunately for my father, Collum's family had stationed a land wight in the way.

1

But Damien still got away with a magical Key that fits a door behind which is a Tool of Ultimate Destruction. We assumed, when he headed to Ireland, that that was where the door was. Haha no – we've since learned that there are four Keys, one for each Element. The Water Key was what he got in West Virginia. The Earth Key was in Ireland, in County Kilkenny, and Collum's father was in charge of guarding it. Which should have made it easy for us to protect, right?

Once Damien got to Ireland, he tried to pull the same con he had in West Virginia. He promised the moon and the stars to the operator of a peat processing plant in County Kilkenny in exchange for helping him find the Earth Key.

The four of us managed to dodge Damien and the thing riding him – it's a demon, by the way, named Surgat, which means "He Who Opens All Locks" – as well as the golems brought to life by the demon, in order to get the Key to safekeeping. Except the new hidey hole didn't turn out to be as safe as we thought it was. Surgat snatched the Key out from under our noses.

Meanwhile, we managed to make the fae mad at us. Although the Tuatha de Danaan are on our side. So are the world's river spirits. As far as I know, that's the sum total of our allies.

And on a personal note, I learned while we were in Ireland that Collum is not quite five hundred years old. Although because he's a gnome, he's really only thirty-five. Or so he tells me. I'm still getting used to the idea.

Anyway, now Daddy Dearest is on his way to Hawaii to find the Fire Key, and we are right behind him. And we really, really hope our luck has changed.

CHAPTER 1 – FRIDAY, IN TRANSIT

A sorrier set of superheroes had never graced an airport waiting area.

At least on the flight from Washington, D.C., to Dublin, half of the team had been excited about flying. Collum the gnome gritted his teeth when he wasn't sleeping, and Your Devoted Undine here spent the whole trip wishing she'd been *in* the ocean instead of tens of thousands of feet above it. But Gail, our sylph, was in her Element in the sky, and Rufus the salamander was all about the rocket power.

Even Collum and I were kind of excited about the trip to Ireland – Collum because he was going to see his parents and me because I'd never been to Ireland. It was supposed to be half-vacation, half-adventure.

Then it turned to a full-on shitshow. My father, Damien Jones, possessed by a demon named Surgat, had nabbed the Water Key before he'd even arrived in Ireland. Then he snatched the Earth Key out from under Collum's parents' cottage, which was totally rude. But at least he didn't destroy Collum's mother's stash of home-canned food when he grabbed it.

So here we were, getting ready to try to beat Surgat to Key Number Three. We hung our hopes on the belief that we could still stop him. He needed all four Elemental Keys for his nefarious plan, and we knew, more or less, where they were: the Fire Key was in Hawaii and the Air Key was in Colorado. We were pretty sure that was more than Surgat knew – but that didn't guarantee a thing. So far, in the battle over the future existence of the Earth, our nameless superhero team was batting zero.

And we still didn't have costumes, which *really* annoyed me.

"So let's say we did get t-shirts," I said. The others groaned, but I pushed on. Anything to take our minds off the mess we'd made of things so far. "What color should they be?"

"Elemental colors, of course," Gail declared, rallying. "Collum's would be green, yours would be blue, and Rufus's would be red."

"What color would yours be?" I asked. "Yellow?"

"Pink, like the dawn," Collum said.

"No way!" I said, shaking my head at him. "Pink is too close to red."

"Tie-dyed," said Collum. "So we each have all the colors."

"I know," Rufus rasped. "Let's get mud brown for everyone, to match our eyes." We'd all had different colored eyes until the mysterious ceremony in the Aether where we'd exchanged Elemental juices. Now all of us had hazel eyes.

That ceremony wasn't as much fun as it sounds.

We all heard the muffled announcement, but Gail was the first to make it out. "That's our flight," she said, wincing as she got up. "Wow. Did we sit here for very long? I shouldn't be this stiff."

Rufus had been dangling his long legs over the arm of the chair next to him. He untangled himself and stood. "Let's get this show on the road. Again."

"Oh, come on, you guys," I said. "Hawaii will be fun. It'll be paradise compared to Ireland."

"Hey, watch it," Collum said, brow lowered.

"Palm trees," I said, deliberately ignoring him. "Blue skies and gentle breezes. And the beach!" I shut my eyes in rapturous contemplation.

"Move it, Raney," Rufus said. "The quicker we get on the plane, the quicker you'll be in those dancing waves."

I sighed, my eyes still shut and a smile on my face. "And between now and then, we get to fly in style." Despite my dwindling bank account, I'd sprung for business class seats for the four of us. I was *not* going to sit up in coach on an eighteen-hour flight. I wanted an actual bed – or what passed for an actual bed on an aircraft without paying through the nose for a private suite like that guy in *Crazy Rich Asians*. Business class seats lie flat. That was good enough for me.

Collum tugged at my sleeve. "Come on, hula girl," he said. "We're boarding."

It turned out that the seats were super nice, with tons of comfy bedding and a serious amount of privacy. The only thing I didn't like was there was no way for Collum and me to sit together. On the other hand, I had more room than the one-third of a twin-size mattress that I'd gotten when we had shared a bed at his parents' house in County Kilkenny. You win some, you lose some.

Partway through the flight, I got up and wandered to the bar. Rufus beckoned to me from his seat at the far end. "Couldn't sleep, or didn't try?" I asked as I slid in next to him. His red hair wasn't any more tousled than it usually was during the day.

"Didn't try," he confirmed. "I'm not really tired yet. You?"

"I had a nap, but I'm too keyed up, I think."

"Yeah." He swirled the brown liquid in the bottom of his glass and swigged it. "So. This Fire Key we're after."

I nodded. "Do you know anything about it?"

"Of course not. And I'm a little tired of the way your man there has been playing his cards close to his vest." He gestured toward the cabin where Collum was presumably sleeping. Rufus had a habit of breaking into a Lucky-Charms-style brogue when referring to him.

My eyes narrowed. "You think he knew about the Earth Key all along?" Collum's father Niall Barth had been charged with guarding the Key. On one hand, it seemed unlikely that Niall hadn't imparted *some* knowledge about the Key to his sons over the centuries. On the other hand... "He's not that great an actor, Rufus."

He smiled sardonically and tipped his glass in my direction. "You have a point there." He downed the rest of his drink.

"Still," I said. "I wish we had more information."

"Well," said Rufus, suppressing a burp, "we know the location has to do with a volcano, and right now there's only one island with active volcanoes."

"Which is why we're headed to the Big Island." I said this regretfully.

"Sounds like you've been there before."

"To Hawaii? Of course," I said. "Although I usually I get a hotel on Waikiki with the rest of the tourists." This time, though, our itinerary would keep us away from the beach in favor of smoking lava pits and black, blasted rock. "Have you ever been?"

"Nope. First time."

"Really? Seems like a natural fit for you."

He shrugged. "It's been on my bucket list, but I never seem to have the money. And when I have money, I don't have the time." He rolled his empty glass between his hands. "I have family there, too. Cousins."

"How cool," I said. "Are you going to try to meet up with them while we're there?"

"No." He set down the glass. "Think I'll try to get a little shuteye. See you later, Raney."

"Later," I said to his retreating back. Then I shrugged. Families are messy, as I knew firsthand. Whatever had occurred between Rufus and his Hawaii relatives was no business of mine.

I mean, I still wanted to know. But I wasn't going to pester him into telling me.

Collum came through the doorway then. I waved him over. "Did you see Rufus?" I asked. "He was just here."

"I did," he confirmed. "He seems upset. Two beers," he said to the bartender. "Guinness if you've got it."

"What if I don't want one?" I said with a lazy smile.

"Who said one of them's for you?" he retorted. Then he kissed me.

I returned the kiss happily. Then I remembered my conversation with our Madman. "So what do *you* know about the Fire Key?" I asked with a lopsided grin.

"Not a thing," he said, handing me a glass of beer. "Cheers." We clinked glasses and drank. "Why do you ask?"

"Something Rufus said."

"So that's what's eating him." He glanced back toward the doorway. "He thinks I'm holding out on the team, just because Da's one of the guardians." He paused. "Or he was." He propped his elbows on the bar and took another gulp of his drink.

I put my hand on his shoulder. "I know this has all been tough on you. First losing your brother, and then the mess with the Key."

He snorted a laugh. "To be honest, Raney, I'm glad I have no personal connection to any of the rest of this. I'm kind of tired of getting kicked in the teeth every time I turn around." He gave me a sidelong look. "Not that it wouldn't suck if we didn't stop your father. But it won't be personal. You know?"

I wrapped an arm around his broad shoulders and laid my cheek on his arm. "I know."

He kissed my forehead. "Drink your beer before it gets warm," he said. "They're too bloody expensive up here to waste."

A couple of beers later, with a pleasant buzz, I headed back to my seat. On the way, I passed Gail's. I would have stopped in to exchange a few words with her, but her seat was down and her lights were out. "Sweet dreams," I whispered to our sylph, and kept going.

It seemed like I'd just gone to sleep when the stewardess called my name. "Ms. Meadows? We'll be serving breakfast soon. Would you like some coffee?"

I slipped off my sleep mask and managed a smile for her. "Sure."

"Say," she said. "Are you the real Raney Meadows?"

I smiled wider while resisting the urge to paw at my hair. I was sure it looked anything but starlet-like. "That's me."

"I just love your show," she said.

It's not mine any more. I'd been let go about three weeks before, after my exploits in Harpers Ferry, West Virginia, made the tabloids. The producers must have been looking for a reason to cut me loose — they hadn't even been interested in hearing that I really *had* been hiking the Appalachian

Trail, and the whole finding-a-dead-body thing was an unfortunate turn of fate. But I kept smiling for the stewardess and offered to get a selfie with her before we landed – after I'd had a chance to comb my hair.

We had to change planes at Los Angeles International Airport. Despite all the technological breakthroughs humanity has achieved, we have yet to develop a passenger jet that can fly from Europe to Hawaii without running out of fuel.

Home, I thought as I stepped off the jetway and into the gate area. LAX is my home airport. I've flown in and out of it so many times that I had to stop myself from heading down the hall to baggage claim and out to a waiting Uber. This time, I reminded myself, we were only changing planes.

And yet I yearned for my beach house, with its pool overlooking the ocean. Mam and I moved a lot when I was a kid, running from my father. Then there was college, where I lived in a dorm the whole time, and a few years of short-term rentals and sofa surfing before I got the *Story of a Homicide* role. I'd never spent a whole year living in one place until I bought the house in Malibu. In a lot of ways, it was the only real home I'd ever had.

We'd just been through a brutal few weeks. I wanted to stop at home and relax. Take a shower. Grab a drink and watch the sun sink into the water, all gold and pink and purple, at the end of the day. But we only had two hours between planes – not nearly enough time.

Sighing, I turned toward my companions and we headed for our connecting flight to Honolulu.

Business class on this flight didn't have the posh lie-flat seats – just the usual roomier-than-economy seats. That meant I could sit next to Collum, which made me happy. But nothing would console him. "How long is this flight again?" he asked me as we settled in.

"About six hours, maybe?"

He groaned. We'd already been traveling for almost nineteen from the time we left Kilkenny. "And then how long to Hilo?"

"Another hour-ish. Are you all right?"

"No. But I'll manage." Then I heard him mutter, "As if I have a choice. After this trip, I'm never leaving solid ground again."

I totally got it. We didn't have window seats this time, and for that I was grateful. I was already having enough trouble, being so close to home but not having time to stop in. If I'd seen us fly over it, there's no telling what I would do. A dive from that high up might have killed me, but I might have risked it anyway.

This time, it was Gail who I ran into during the flight. "Got your beauty sleep on the other leg?" I said with a grin. (We'd left Dublin at three in the afternoon. It had been dinner time when we got to LAX.)

She smiled. "I'm in the habit of catching a nap whenever I can. You never know when you'll get another chance."

"Yeah, but an eighteen-hour nap?"

"I didn't sleep the whole time," she said. I waited for more, but that was all she said.

I tried another avenue of attack. "Is this your first trip to Hawaii?"

"Nope. I used to fly through Honolulu pretty regularly on my way to Asia."

"For work."

"Right."

I couldn't help adding, "On a plane?"

She grinned. "Planes are faster, even for a sylph."

I conceded the point. "I can't swim as fast as a plane can fly, either."

"There you go." She went on, "So do you think Damien will beat us there?"

That was a fair question. "I think he's beaten us to Hawaii," I said. He had at least a day's head start on us. "But I'm not convinced he knows exactly where to go."

"That's what I think, too. From what I saw in the peat plant office, until he met up with Dermot Phelan, he had no idea where to begin looking." Phelan was the owner of the plant. Damien had offered him a lot of money in exchange for helping him find the Key.

"We're not much better off," I said. "In or near a volcano is all we've got."

"Ah," she said. "But we have friends, and he has none."

"Friends?" I echoed. "Like what kind of friends?"

"Ask Rufus," she said.

So I wandered over to the Madman's seat. "Gail says you have friends in Hawaii," I said.

He scowled. "Windy needs to keep her mouth shut." He looked at me, hard. "And you, Torrent, need to quit stirring shit up."

My eyes widened. "Me? You're the one who was mad at Collum for no good reason!"

He turned his gaze to the window and said nothing more.

I threw up my hands and went back to my seat — and just in time, too, as the seatbelt sign came on for landing. "This is gonna be a swell trip," I said to no one in particular.

Collum, looking green, reached for the barf bag.

"Yup," I said, rubbing his shoulder. "It's gonna be super-dee-duper."

CHAPTER 2 – THE FOREVER FRIDAY

Time zones suck. We had left Dublin at three in the afternoon and traveled for twenty-five hours, yet it was still Friday when we landed in Honolulu. It was too late to catch a flight to the Big Island, so we got a room at a hotel near Honolulu International Airport.

Back when we were making the reservations, we'd agreed to a day of rest on Oahu, even though it gave Damien another day to look for the Key without us. I lobbied briefly for the North Shore – bigger waves and much less touristy than Waikiki – but then I remembered what had happened the last time I was there. A typhoon had hit the island, knocking out power and grounding flights for a day, and then I lost another day trying to get a seat on any flight back to LAX. I'd lost an acting job because of the delay – and Sid, my erstwhile agent, had thrown that in my face when he fired me by phone when I was in Harpers Ferry.

"Never mind," I'd told the gang. "Waikiki's fine with me."

"I'd rather stay near the airport," Gail said, and Rufus agreed.

"It's not that far from the airport," I said, "and we'd be near the beach."

I guess I should have kept the last part to myself. As soon as the others heard it, they said no. Even though they got part of me in the transfer. Jerks.

Anyway, the less said about our first night in Hawaii, the better. Travel makes people cranky and we'd done a ton of it over the past couple of weeks. We muttered good night to each other and headed for our rooms.

Collum couldn't sleep. After he jostled me awake from turning over for about the fourth time, I blurted, "Are you okay over there?"

"No," he said with a sigh, and flipped onto his back. "I can't bear the thought of getting on another plane."

That had been bothering me, too. I told him what I'd been telling myself: "It'll be a very short flight."

"I know that," he said. Then after a few seconds, he said, "Maybe you guys could do this part without me."

"Sorry, dude. It's all for one and one for all, or whatever the saying is." I said it lightly, but inside I was panicking – and I could feel it starting to boil over.

He sighed again and reached for my hand. Then he dropped it and turned over, his back to me.

Maybe if I focused on helping Collum, it would keep me from turning into a screaming mess. "Hey," I said, getting up on one elbow. "What do you usually do ground yourself?"

"My feet are always on the ground."

I punched his shoulder. "You know what I mean. Like how I go for a soak. What do you do?"

"Nothing. I told you – I'm always grounded."

I looked around our hotel room – functional but impersonal, and four stories up. "Well, you're not grounded *here*. Come on." I swung my legs over my side of the bed and flipped on the reading light. Then I began pulling on my pants and t-shirt from the previous day.

He sat up and looked at me in disbelief. "Now? We're supposed to be sleeping, Raney."

"This will help, I promise."

Grumbling, he rolled out of bed and got dressed. Then he allowed me to lead him downstairs and out the back door of the hotel.

It wasn't a resort, which is to say there wasn't much in the way of grounds around it. But it did have an outdoor pool with a little landscaping surrounding it. I ignored the signs about pool hours and swimming at your own risk, swiped my keycard, and pushed open the gate. "Here we go," I said. "We both need this worse than sleep right now."

"I should have brought my swimsuit," he said.

12

"You're not going in the pool. You're going to sit over … here." I spied a spot of dirt in amongst the tropical plants ringing the pool area.

"I don't get a chair?" he asked.

"This is medicinal," I told him. "Sit down."

He shrugged and dropped, cross-legged, between a couple of ferns. "These things sure grow big around here," he said, eyeing the plants as if one of them would devour him. Then he looked up at me. "Go on. Get in the water. I'll be fine."

I bent to kiss the top of his head. Then I kicked off my flip-flops and sat on the edge of the pool. I resolved not to go to pieces in my usual way – the area was too public, what with some of the hotel rooms overlooking it. Also, I was sure hotel security had a camera trained on the pool, and probably also sent someone by periodically. Plus the pool chemicals made the water less than ideal for my purposes. You haven't lived 'til you've been purified with chlorine at the cellular level. Don't ask me how I know.

None of my rationalizations mattered. Once I was submerged, my stressed-out body did what it needed to do. Particles of me could feel my clothes drifting away. I made a few waves to move them into the shadows, and then I gave myself up to the Water.

Cleansed and replenished – and reeking of chlorine, both inside and outside – I reassembled and drifted into the shadows where my sopping wet clothes floated. I wrung them out and donned them hurriedly, hoping Security wasn't watching. Then I went to check on Collum.

He was stretched out on the dirt, fast asleep.

I didn't have the heart to wake him. Instead I settled myself on the nearest lounge chair and waited for sunrise.

Much later, he woke me with a kiss. "Come on, sleeping beauty. Let's go upstairs."

I roused myself. As the day brightened, the lights around the pool blinked out. "I didn't mean to fall asleep," I said, stretching.

"Neither did I." He pulled me up and encircled me with his arms. "Thanks. You were right. I needed that."

I grinned. "Doctor Raney to the rescue. I bet I can do something about another problem you're having, too." I wiggled my hips a little.

"Keep that up and we'll both be naked in the pool," he said.

"Wouldn't be the first time," I said. But then we heard voices. Hotel staff, probably. I made a pouty face. "Well, phooey."

"There *is* a perfectly good bed upstairs," he reminded me, as he led me to the gate.

It was a perfectly good bed, and we ended up barely having enough time to shower, dress, and repack before meeting the others for breakfast.

Gail grinned when she saw us. "You two look like you had a good night."

"Very restful," Collum confirmed, with a sly look at me.

A good night's sleep had done Rufus a world of good. His surly travel manner was gone and he was back to being a ball of energy. "I'll feel better once we get to the Big Island," he said. "Can't wait to get up close and personal with a volcano or two. When's our flight again?"

I felt Collum stiffen at the mention of the upcoming flight. "It'll be short," I reminded him.

Rufus looked at Collum's plate. "Lost your appetite, Leprechaun?" he asked hopefully.

"No," said Collum, and resumed eating.

"So what are we doing today?" I said, changing the subject.

"Let's tour the Arizona," Rufus said. The U.S.S. Arizona was one of the United States' first naval casualties in World War II. The Japanese dragged us into the war by bombing the Pearl Harbor naval base in Honolulu. In the bombardment, the Arizona and some other ships sank. Instead of salvaging them, the Navy left them there and built a memorial over the top of the Arizona.

I wrinkled my nose. "Aren't there dead sailors inside the ship still?"

"Yeah," Rufus said, his eyes alight.

"Rufus," I said. "Why do you keep trying to drag me to places where people have died?"

"I don't…"

"Kilmainham Gaol," I reminded him.

"Oh," he said. "Yeah. But it's not *deliberate*."

"Of course not," I said. I knew he was telling the truth – I just wanted him to start thinking about what he was saying before he opened his mouth. As if. "Just the same, I'll pass," I said. "Gail?"

"I'm thinking of heading up to Diamond Head," she said.

Collum perked up. "Hiking or flying?"

"I could hike, if you want to come along," she said.

He looked apologetically at me. "Sorry. I'm not much for the beach."

Flustered, I said, "I might not want to go to the …"

"Right," he said, laughing.

"Fine, then. I'll go to the beach myself." And so I did. We all called our respective Ubers and parted ways.

Waikiki Beach was just as I remembered it: liberally supplied with palm trees, sand, turquoise waters, and tourists. I found a spot that wasn't quite wall-to-wall beach towels and set up camp. Then I shucked my coverup and went into the water.

I was relieved I'd gone to pieces in the hotel pool the night before, or I surely would have done it here.

Collum had asked me once where my home water was. I put him off because I didn't really have one – Mam and I had moved so often that I never had a chance to put down Watery roots anywhere. But since I'd bought that beach house in Malibu, the ocean – specifically the Pacific Ocean – was my jam.

The Pacific was calm on this beautiful day, the sun warm on my face. I lay back and let the waves rock me, tossing me this way and that.

Then I felt a gentle poke.

Then, after a moment, another poke.

And after another moment, something poked me harder.

"Collum?" I said, jackknifing and treading water. But he wasn't there. Nobody was there. Or at least nobody was near me in the water.

I looked toward the beach and went cold all over. A hulking figure dressed in a dark suit plodded along the shingle. Then it turned a little inland. It looked to me like it was heading for my towel.

Surgat must have left a golem behind to watch for our arrival.

The clay creatures, I knew, were impervious to water. It could wade right in after me. I could dodge it by dissolving, but then I'd lose my swimsuit. And I'd have to reassemble at some point.

Scared witless, I stayed put, watching the thing as it cruised past my towel and kept going. Plod, plod, plod, heading north along the shingle.

I felt another poke and looked down. A sea turtle had surfaced next to me and regarded me with ancient, unblinking eyes. Once it had my attention, it swam ahead of me toward the sand. It stopped and turned; seeing me still unmoving, it came back and jostled my elbow with its nose. Then it turned and went back toward the beach.

That shook me from my stasis. I struck out with powerful strokes born of fear. When the water got too shallow for swimming, I turned to the turtle. "Thanks," I said.

Apparently satisfied, it turned around and swam away.

I grabbed up my stuff and ran.

Collum found me in the bathtub of our room. I'd shed my suit as soon as I got the door shut and dove into the safest thing I knew, coming apart as soon as the tub had a few inches of water in it.

"It's safe," he said. "You can come out."

With an effort, I pulled my head together. "Are you sure?"

"Gail saw it from the air. She's tracking it."

I nodded. "Which of you told the turtle to warn me?"

He frowned and cocked his head. "Turtle?"

"Yeah. A sea turtle poked me to get me to notice the thing. Then it told me when it was safe to go back to shore."

He shook his head. "That wasn't due to either of us." He smiled. "Looks like you made a friend."

"I guess." Suddenly I needed Collum more than I needed the comfort of Water. I reassembled and reached for him, bursting into tears.

Rufus had seen a golem, too. He told us about it as we ate dinner at a seafood place down the road from the hotel. "It was creepy," he said. "The thing was sitting in the weeds across from the entrance to the Arizona Memorial. Looked like a Buddha statue, kind of, until you saw the dead eyes and the suit."

"Surgat must have left scouts in Honolulu," I said. "Keeping track of us."

"Did you have any luck?" Collum said to Gail.

She shook her head ruefully. "It walked into one of the resorts and seemed to disappear. Wish I'd had a tracker to put on it."

"A tracker?" Collum asked.

"Yeah, you know. A bug. An electronic device. Like…" She must have remembered who she was talking to, because all of a sudden her lips snapped shut.

After a moment of stunned silence, Rufus resumed where we'd left off. "Maybe that golem hunkered down and made like a statue, like the one I saw."

"Maybe." Gail shrugged. "I like to think I would have noticed, though. I hope I'm not losing my touch."

"I doubt it," Collum said. "I think it accomplished what it was meant to do."

"Scare us, you mean?" I shivered. "It sure scared me. Do you think we should change our plans at all?"

"Why would we?" Gail asked.

"Well, my father knows where we are now. He must know we're heading for the Big Island."

"Which is where he is," she said. "The golems didn't threaten either of you, right? So they were simply lookouts. Damien already knew we were coming – he left the golems here so he would know when we arrived. I don't think anything has changed."

Collum nodded in agreement. "Right. He's been keeping an eye on us since Dublin."

"Let's fly to Hilo in the morning, as we'd planned," Gail said.

I sighed. "I guess so. I mean, our only alternative is to stay here longer – which gives him more time to look for the Key without us."

"Exactly."

"In a way," Rufus said, "it's good to know Damien left those golems here to track us. It means he considers us a threat."

I swallowed hard. The thought didn't give me as much comfort as Rufus meant it to.

That night, Collum and I talked it over, and came to the same conclusion we had at dinner – nothing had changed and we needed to keep going.

"So how was your day, anyway?" I asked. "Before Gail flew away, I mean."

"Good. It's a beautiful hike, although the trail was crowded. Everybody and his brother does that ascent to Diamond Head." He laughed softly. "I've seen the A.T. crowded, but not like this."

We'd met just off the Appalachian Trail, near where I'd found his brother's body in the Shenandoah River.

"Gail's good at getting people to talk," he went on. "She asked me a bunch of stuff about my family."

"Anything I should know?"

He kissed my forehead. "I've already told you all of it. I just hadn't talked about it with anyone else."

"I think she's gotten Rufus talking, too, a little," I said.

"She's becoming our mother confessor."

"We probably need one." I raised my head to look at him. "I wonder who's going to be her confessor, though. Remember when we were talking about how Rufus had gotten your anger at your parents in the transfer, and she wondered whether he'd gotten her anger, too?"

He nodded. "She wouldn't tell us what she was angry about, either."

"Nope. And she still hasn't." I rested my head on his shoulder again. "I think I'll try to get her to confess."

He laughed. "Good luck with that."

CHAPTER 3 – SATURDAY WITH A SMOKING VOLCANIC PIT

The flight to Hilo was short and uneventful. As we made our way to baggage claim, Rufus gazed out across the airfield. "Man, this airport is small. I don't think I've ever been in one so small."

I only half heard him. I had my radar out for my father – the airport *was* small and I didn't want to be surprised by him, or any of Surgat's golems, for that matter. Gail gave me a questioning look. "Nobody's here," I said in relief.

She confirmed it with a nod. "But remember, Damien may have flown into Kona."

We'd talked about this when we made our reservations. We knew the Fire Key was in Hawaii and that its location had something to do with a volcano, which wasn't as helpful as it could have been – the island chain was created by volcanoes. The Big Island had five volcanic peaks. Mauna Loa and Mauna Kea both topped thirteen thousand feet; next in height was Hualalai, then Kohala, and then Kilauea. Kilauea was the baby at nearly forty-one-thousand feet, but it was also the one that had erupted most recently. We all remembered seeing spectacular video of lava pouring off a cliff and into a steaming sea.

Rufus had persuaded us that the Fire Key would be nearest the fire, as it were – although the guardians moved the keys around and sometimes the current location wasn't the most logical one, as we'd discovered in Ireland. But still, the Big Island was the most logical place to focus our search.

The island had two airports, though: Hilo on the east side and Kona-Kailua on the west side. Hilo was closer to Volcanoes National Park, which included Kilauea and Mauna Loa. If the Fire Key were hidden near the most active volcano on the island, flying into Hilo made the most sense. But Gail argued that Damien might still think he needed a cover story for his search for the Key. And if he were playing at being a real estate developer, he'd want to be near the biggest resorts, which were on the northern and western shores of the island. For those, Kona was the closest airport.

Finally, we flipped a coin – heads, Kona; tails, Hilo. Tails it was.

As we collected our baggage, Collum asked, "You think he might be watching the other airport and not this one?"

"Seems to me a smart demon would set a watch on both," Rufus said. He grabbed Gail's suitcase and handed it to her.

"He opens all locks," I said, keeping an eye on my ginormous backpack as it approached. "Doesn't mean he's smart."

Collum hauled his suitcase off the conveyor belt. "I'll go get the rental car while you guys wait for the rest of the stuff," he said, and headed across the street with his bag in tow.

"Right behind you," Gail said, following.

I nudged Rufus. "Any luck finding out her secret?"

"Nope." He snagged my backpack straps and handed it over to me. "What's in this thing, anyway? It weighs a ton."

I laughed as I strapped it on. "What are you talking about? It's feather-light. I ditched all the really heavy gear before we got to Dulles."

Gail sprang for our lodgings. I think she saw my grimace when I paid for the business class airline tickets. Or maybe it was when I suggested we stay in a hostel near the national park. Anyway, she went online and booked a place, and then told us about it.

"You didn't need to do that," I'd said.

"Look, Raney," she said. "I may be on a fixed income, but you're unemployed. Let someone else do the heavy lifting for this trip. Okay?"

"Okay," I said. Secretly, though, I was relieved.

So anyway, what we got were rooms in a renovated historic hotel just inside the boundary of Volcanoes National Park. The dining room overlooked the smoking hot Halema'uma'u Crater – and when I say *smoking hot*, I mean the crater was actually smoking.

Rufus was beside himself. His room overlooked the crater, too. "I've never been this close to a volcano before," he said, beaming. "This is awesome!" He dropped his stuff in his room and immediately ran outside to goggle at the blasted landscape.

"Don't get so close that your shoes melt," Gail called after him. Then she shook her head in amusement. "He's like a big kid."

"That's our Madman," Collum said. He'd regained what equilibrium he'd lost on the flight over, and once again looked like the fierce mountain gnome I'd grown to love.

We had some time before lunch, so we dragged a reluctant Rufus away from his contemplation of the crater and trekked over to the visitor center. There I found an arresting sight of my own: a painting of Pele, the Hawaiian goddess of volcanoes.

"That's her home out there," Rufus said, startling me. He pointed at the windows behind us.

"What, the crater?"

"Yep. According to Hawaiian mythology, Kilauea is where she lives."

I turned my gaze to the view, such as it was, and back to him. "Has She spoken to you?"

"Not so far. But there's time." He grinned at me.

"Hey, where do your relatives live, anyway? You never said."

"Not here," he said with a laugh. "They're all up on the North Shore of Oahu. And before you ask, they're not Elementals."

"Are they Native Hawaiians?"

"Nope. As far as I know, they're *haole*, like all of us." He twirled a finger to include me and the other team members. "The Hawaiian branch of the family came here in the '60s for the surfing and never left."

"Sounds like the sort of people you'd be related to," I said with a smirk.

"Yep, we're all lazy jerks," he replied cheerfully. "But seriously, I think that's why my mother didn't keep in touch with them. They were a little too counter-culture for her taste."

"Gotcha. So you're Elemental on your dad's side?"

"Exactly. We're Pennsylvania coal miners from way back. Fire is a great talent to have for that – setting charges to blow new seams open and that kind of thing." His gaze drifted to the window. "Volcanoes are several magnitudes greater, though. This is real, raw firepower." He focused on me again. "Hey, let's get going. I'd like to get out into the park. There's a road that circles the crater – we should have time to do that before lunch."

"You're kidding," Gail said as she joined us. "Rufus, putting off a meal? Are you feeling okay?"

"He's jonesing for Pele," Collum said.

"You guys are all assholes. You know that?" Rufus said, but he was smiling. "Come on, let's go. I'll drive."

So we trudged across the road again and got in the rental car. I debated for a moment the wisdom of letting Rufus pilot us – visions of him turning off the main road and across a lava field cavorted through my head – but he was not nearly as crazy behind the wheel as he could have been. I began to relax.

And then, as we headed toward the turnoff for Mauna Loa, I felt a tickle of fear. It was a familiar one, and it wasn't generated by any of us.

Gail, who rode shotgun, looked back at me. "I'm not imagining that, am I?" she said.

"Nope," I confirmed. "Rufus, we need to go back the other way."

He regarded me in the rearview mirror, then executed a U-turn. The farther we were from the intersection, the easier I could breathe.

"So he's here," Collum said.

"I don't think so," Gail said. "I think he's *been* here, but the scent didn't seem recent to me."

23

I thought about that. "Maybe it drifted down from Mauna Loa," I said at last. "But I couldn't tell how old it was."

"I didn't mean it was last week," Gail amended. "Just… If he's here, he passed that way quite some time ago."

"There's only one road to the crest of Mauna Loa," Collum said as he consulted his handy-dandy pocket computer. "If he went that way, he'll be coming back down."

While he spoke, I scanned the area anxiously for animated clay lookouts. "Can we just get out of here?" I said. My emotions go into overdrive at the drop of a hat anyway – it's an undine thing, owing to our affinity to Water – and by this point I was really rattled. I mean, we were just *sitting* there. My father could have overtaken us at any time.

We were almost to the turn for the hotel. "Let's get lunch in town," Gail said. "By the time we're done, hopefully the scent here will dissipate enough so that we can get on with the tour."

Rufus shrugged and kept going. "He could be up there for a while," he said. "There's a whole trail system up in there. He could be hiking for hours."

"Damien Jones doesn't strike me as a hiker," Collum said. "My guess is he'll drive up to the parking lot and let his golems sniff around. If they don't find anything, they'll head back."

"Through town," I squeaked. "And there's only one road."

"We've got you covered, Raney," Rufus said. "I saw the perfect place for an incognito lunch on our way up. Damien wouldn't be caught dead in it – not even to go in and look for us."

I saw what he meant as soon as we got there. The restaurant was little more than a shack. Hand-drawn signs peeked out from among a riot of rainbow whirligigs, advertising PLATE LUNCH and SHAVE ICE – 12 FLAVORS. Tibetan peace flags stretched along the eaves.

"You're right," I said, my anxiety easing. "My father would *never* go in here."

Rufus pulled around to the back and parked. The lot wasn't full, but we weren't the only car, either. The entrance off the parking lot sported another hand-drawn sign, this one declaring we'd arrived at ANNIE'S PLACE.

Opening the door rang a bell hung above the jamb. "Hello!" someone called. "Sit anywhere. I'll be right out." We exchanged shrugs and picked a booth in the far back corner. Collum plucked the menus from their slot behind the napkin holder and passed them around. It didn't take long to figure out what I wanted – there wasn't much offered besides the plate lunch: two scoops of rice, macaroni salad, and your choice of meat. I passed my menu back to Collum and glanced around at the décor: the white paneling was hung with colorful surfboards, carved wooden tiki masks, and leis made out of silk flowers.

A few minutes after we came in, a comfortably padded woman with black hair and merry cheeks emerged from a doorway and scanned the restaurant. "Oh, there you are!" she said, spying us. "Are you hiding from someone?"

Well, yeah, kinda. "Why do you ask?" I said.

"Because most people like the tables by the window. Do you want to move?"

"Nope, we're good right here, thanks," I said.

She peered at me. "Can I ask you something?"

"Sure."

"Because you look exactly like that actress on *Story of a Homicide*." She laughed. "I bet you get that all the time."

I grinned. "I do, yeah."

"So are you … ?"

I nodded. What else was I going to do?

"How wonderful! Maybe we could get a picture later. And you can tell me how much you like the food. We can put it up with the other celebrities who've been here." She gestured behind her, and now I saw a grouping of photos on the wall near the front door. "Would you mind?"

25

"Not at all," I said, still smiling. Although I made a mental note to check out who I'd be hanging next to. Finding out who else people think of as a celebrity can either boost your ego or deflate it, depending.

"So what'll it be?" she asked. "Need more time with the menu?"

"Nope," I said. "The shrimp plate lunch, please."

"I'll have the same, but with teriyaki beef," said Collum.

"Chicken katsu plate lunch," said Gail.

"And you, sir?" our waitress asked. Then her eyes got really big. "Rufus? Rufus MacKay!"

"Hey, Annie," he said with a sheepish grin.

"Well, get over here and give me a hug!" cried Annie. While the reunion hug lasted, the three of us exchanged looks of … fascination, let's call it.

"Sooo," I said when they broke apart, "how do you two know each other?"

"We're cousins," Annie said.

"By marriage," Rufus amended, then turned to Annie. "What are you doing here? Did you finally give Branson the boot?"

Her mouth twisted in a grimace. "You bet I did. He thought I didn't know he was seeing that little girl in the apartment down the way from us. But I knew." She nodded fiercely. "So I told him to pack his bags and get out. Maybe she'd make him get a job finally. But he wouldn't do it – so *I* left. Mom needed the help here, anyway."

"How long ago was that?" he asked, resuming his seat.

She shrugged. "Couple of years. I think they're both living in her car now." She gave us a wicked grin. "Rent's expensive on Oahu. Doesn't take long to run out of money when you won't get a *job*."

Rufus's eyes sparkled as he changed the subject. "Is Auntie here? I'd love to see her."

"Oh, she's at home. But it's not far." Her eyes widened as inspiration struck. "I know! Why don't you all come for supper tonight? It'll give Rufus and me a chance to catch up. Oh!" She whacked herself in the forehead with the heel of her hand. "I'm sorry. I'm Annie Yamamoto. I recognized Ms. Meadows…"

"It's Raney, please," I said. "Any friend of Rufus's is a friend of mine."

"Raney," she said, nodding. "And you other folks are … ?"

"Gail Oleander," Rufus supplied. "And Collum Barth."

"Say, Annie," Collum said, "are you sure you want to invite Rufus for supper? He'll eat you out of house and home."

"Jerk," Rufus said, but he was grinning.

"Oh, I know all about Rufus and his appetite. We go *way* back." Annie looked at him fondly. "Mom will be so happy to see you. Well." She collected herself. "Let me get your orders in. Plate lunch for you, too, Rufus? Kalua pig, right?"

"What else?" he said.

"I'll make sure you get the big plate," she said, "so your friends won't have to guard theirs from you."

As she bustled away, I turned a snarky eye toward Rufus. "Why, she *does* know you," I said.

Diners are the best thing ever, no matter where you find them, and Annie's Place was no exception. The food was tasty and filling, and best of all, she treated us to shave ice for dessert. Shave ice is kind of like a snowcone, but better – the ice is shaved instead of crushed, and the syrups are more fun. Plus you can order interesting things to go under your ice. I had mango syrup with adzuki beans on the bottom. I do love me some adzuki beans.

Annie wanted to comp us the whole meal, but Collum insisted on paying. I followed him up to the register to get the photo with Annie and to check out the wall of fame. I figured they'd be little local luminaries, but I was surprised to see a few honest-to-goodness famous faces endorsing the place. I even knew some of them. That guy was the star of a TV show I'd done a guest appearance on a few months before. I'd done a different show with this woman, and boy, was she ever a diva. And that guy …

Oh. Oh, no.

"Say," Collum said. "Isn't that Stone Wolff?"

"Yeah," I said. "Yeah, it is."

"Do you know him?"

I knew he was looking at me, but I couldn't tear my eyes away from the photo of the asshole with Annie. "Yeah," I said. "Yeah, I do."

"Oh," Annie said, joining us. "You know Stone? What a coincidence. He's here on the Big Island right now."

I tore my eyes away from the photo. "He's *here?*"

"Yeah. He's doing a movie on location, he said."

"*Here?*" I repeated.

"Not *here* here," she said. "Over near Waipio Valley. He told me he had a break in shooting and came to see the volcanoes." She smiled at the photo. "Such a nice guy."

"Yeah," I said. "He's a real peach."

Annie must have heard the edge in my voice, because she mumbled something and beat a retreat.

"Okay," Collum said. "There's a story here. Want to tell me?"

"He's my ex-boyfriend." At Collum's surprised look, I elaborated. "He's the guy who wanted to out me as a curiosity, to make more money for himself." I turned back to the photo, glowering. Now I had two men I needed to avoid – and I didn't think the island was big enough for all three of us.

Chapter 4 – Still Saturday, but with Home Cooking

"I guess I should have called Mom and gotten an update on the fam," Rufus said. While I was still preoccupied with alternating feelings of anxiety and rage, he blathered on about stumbling across his cousin-by-marriage. "I've always liked Annie. Bran's the one I was trying to avoid. He was such an asshole to me."

"Guess he was an asshole to Annie, too," Gail said. That almost shook me from my reverie – Gail hardly ever swore.

Rufus snorted. "Since the beginning. I couldn't figure out why she married him in the first place. She and her mother came out to visit after they got engaged, and I saw then how he treated her." He shook his head. "Anyway, Auntie Helen is a lot of fun. You guys are gonna love her." He looked around. Then he said quietly, as if there might be someone other than us in the car to hear it, "She really gets the Elemental thing."

"Is she … ?" That was Gail.

"No!" Rufus laughed. "No, not at all. She's Native Hawaiian with a side of Japanese. But she was raised on the old Hawaiian religion, so she knows a lot about the mystical creatures who inhabit the islands." He turned to me. "We should ask her about your sea turtle, Raney."

"Sure," I said.

Collum had been holding my hand ever since we left the restaurant. "Are you okay?" he asked.

I drew a ragged breath. "Nope. But it's fine."

Gail threw me a skeptical look. Then she turned to the guys. "How do we find out more about that film crew?"

"I should have thought of that," said Collum, and fished his phone out of his pocket with his free hand. After a minute or two, he gave up. "The signal's terrible here. I'll have to wait 'til we get back to the hotel."

"Maybe the front desk will know something," Rufus offered.

"Good idea," Gail said. "I'll ask when we get back. If we can manage to stay away from them, I think it will be easier on Raney."

"Thanks, Gail," I said gratefully.

"Of course," she said. "We're a team. Anything we can do to ease each other's burdens, we ought to do it without even thinking about it."

We made a quick pit stop at the hotel. Then with some trepidation, we got back in the car and headed out to finish the crater rim tour we'd aborted in the morning.

I held my breath as we approached the turn off for Mauna Loa – but the whiff of evil I'd gotten earlier in the day had dissipated. I exhaled and almost smiled. "Whatever it was," I said, "it's gone now."

"Maybe it wasn't Damien," Collum said.

My eyebrows shot up. "What else could it have been?"

He shrugged. "No idea. I'm just saying that we haven't seen or heard or felt anything else that we could attribute to him since we arrived. No golems, no sightings, no nothing. So maybe whatever you ladies sensed this morning was something other than him."

I side-eyed him. "Thanks a lot. Just what I need – something new to worry about."

We didn't get much farther past the Mauna Loa turnoff before we had to stop. The most recent eruption of Kilauea had so badly destabilized Crater Rim Drive that the road ahead of us was closed.

"Well, damn," Rufus said. "There's supposed to be a museum over this way, and a spectacular overlook."

"Not anymore," said Gail, consulting a pamphlet she'd picked up at the visitor center. "The museum is closed until further notice, and the volcano ate the overlook."

I blinked. "*Ate* the overlook? Like, literally?"

"Literally. The crater's a lot wider now, and the parking lot fell into it."

"Wow. Okay. Is the road open back the other way?"

"Yeah." Rufus looked regretfully at the big ROAD CLOSED sign in front of us. "But we can't complete the circle."

"You're not going to try to do it on foot, are you?" Gail said sharply. "A whole bunch of the trails are closed, too."

Rufus didn't answer. He just turned the car around.

We parked later, at a trailhead on the other side of the crater. "Let's take a walk," Rufus said, and was out of the car before the rest of us had our seatbelts undone.

The trail he'd chosen took us to an overlook on the opposite side of the crater from the one the volcano ate. I could see it was perfectly safe and stable, but still, we were almost closer to the crater than I wanted to be. Steam rose from fissures along the sides of the broken, ash-colored land. The signage hadn't been updated since the last eruption and the photos didn't at all match what we were seeing.

"It would be cool to come back in a few decades," Rufus said. "Just to see how things change. Maybe Kilauea will erupt again in the meantime."

"You *want* another eruption? Really? This last one gobbled up seven hundred homes," Gail said.

Rufus turned to her, glassy-eyed. The human toll hadn't occurred to him at all. Not that he was an uncaring person — he did feel for others, in his way. But the volcano had grabbed our Madman and would not spit him out any time soon.

"I wonder how long it will take for the land to recover," Collum said quietly.

"You okay?" I asked. "This must be pretty hard for you to look at — all this destruction."

He shrugged. "It happens," he said. "Sometimes Fire destroys Earth. Sometimes it covers Earth in ash, or new rock bubbles up from Earth's depths." He inclined his head toward me. "Volcanoes are of the Earth, too, you know."

"I suppose that's true. I never thought about it before."

We all stood silently for a few more minutes. Then a noisy group of hikers came down into the overlook, breaking the spell. Rufus sighed and, with one last look, turned back toward the trail.

We got out of the car a few more times that afternoon. We hiked down into a section of rainforest, which was wild – all that moisture! – and out to a petroglyph.

And then we reached the end of the road. Literally. Once it had been a two-lane road all the way to Hilo, but lava from an eruption in the 1970s had completely covered it to a height of several feet. We lined up against the uneven surface and prevailed upon another tourist to take our picture. Then, as Rufus and Collum scrambled up and over the cooled rock, I drifted toward the cliff edge and looked down to the sea. A rock – not volcanic rock, or not recent volcanic rock anyway – jutted out into the ocean here, and over time, the waves had eroded a hole through it.

Gail walked up and stood next to me. "A sea arch," she said. "Water is stronger than rock."

"Eventually," I said with a smile. "Air's quicker. Spin up a hurricane and shove something right through it."

She planted her feet a shoulders' width apart, clasped her hands behind her back, and stared out to sea. The breeze blew softly through her hair. "Some days I could just take off, you know?" she said. "Just fly away and never …"

I gave her time to finish the sentence, but she didn't. "You wouldn't, though," I said. "You wouldn't leave forever. You'd come back."

"Damn my sense of duty anyhow," she said ruefully.

I put my arm around her waist. She didn't reciprocate the hug, but she didn't shake me off, either.

"We should go find the guys," I said after a few minutes. But I discovered as I turned that there was no need – they were already rejoining us.

"Have you seen anything that could be a marker?" Rufus asked, bringing us back to the task at hand. Both in Harpers Ferry and in Kilkenny, there had been a stone marker pointing toward the place where the Keys were hidden. It stood to reason that some sort of similar ancient feature would point toward the Fire Key's hidey-hole.

"No," I said. "Unless you count the sea arch."

"Yeah, probably not that," Collum said. "We were wondering just now whether the marker might have been covered up by the latest eruption."

Gail's eyes widened. "That would be distinctly unhelpful. Did your father give you any information about the guardian of this Key?"

"Like maybe who they are and where we can find them?" Rufus asked.

Collum shook his head. "No. The impression I got was that they don't know who's in charge now. They were friends with the guardians in Spain, but those folks didn't move here with the Key, and now they've lost touch. Mam's worried their friends in Spain are dead."

"I hope not," I said, empathetic for their loss.

Rufus's lip curled, but he remained silent. Which was probably a good thing, given that he thought the Barths were holding out on us.

"Well," Gail said, "this has all been very educational, but we're no closer to finding the Key. And the dinner hour is approaching. Why don't we head back to the hotel and freshen up?"

"Sounds like a plan," Collum said. "And I'll see if I can find any more information on the film crew." He shot a look at me that I had trouble interpreting – which wasn't usually a problem for me. I figured it had something to do with the ex, whose name I still didn't want to say. No sense in calling evil to me, if there was any way around it.

Calling evil... "I wonder if it was the ex whose presence I felt this morning," I mused aloud.

Gail stared at me. "Is he as evil as Surgat?"

I considered that. "Maybe. Or maybe I just think he is."

I had no idea how to dress to meet Rufus's relatives by marriage. Everything seemed so laid back here, but still. Finally, I opted for a sundress and sandals I'd picked up on Oahu. The sundress was blue with cartoony hibiscus flowers all over it. I wasn't a huge fan of hibiscus, but the other option had been a tiki-head-and-coconut print. Not only was that one ugly, but it had the potential to rile up the local spirits, and we were going to need their help.

"Nice," Collum said when he saw me. "Very nice." He'd opted for jeans and a polo shirt.

"You look very nice, too," I said. "I think we'll pass muster with the fam."

He grinned and offered me an elbow. I wrapped my hands around it and we set out to meet the others in the lobby.

Gail was in one of her billowy-sleeved tops and a pair of capris. Rufus had swapped the t-shirt he'd worn all day for a clean one.

Eyeing him, I whispered to Collum, "That answers whether we needed to dress up."

He grinned at me. "I'll drive," he announced. "You can navigate, Rufus."

"Fine," he said, and pushed open the hotel door.

It was a quick trip from the hotel to Annie's home in Volcano Village. I expected another shack, but no – her single-story rambler wouldn't have looked out of place in a suburb anywhere in America. "Come on in," she cried when she met us at the door. "Mom's out back. I already told her you were coming. She's so excited to see you all."

The kitchen smelled amazing as we trooped through it to the backyard. Rufus went out the back door first and greeted Annie's mother with an enthusiastic hug. Mrs. Yamamoto was tiny, and looked as frail as her daughter looked robust. Her hair was a gorgeous snow white.

"You look great, Auntie," Rufus said.

"Thank you, Rufus. I am glad to see you looking so well," she said. "And you have friends!" That got a laugh. "Introduce me," she ordered, and so he did.

When he got to me, Mrs. Yamamoto took my hand and held it firmly in hers. "It's such a pleasure to meet you. I'm your biggest fan. I've seen everything you've ever done. Even that horrible movie with the dead tree. Wasn't it horrible, Annie?"

Annie's face was wreathed in smiles. "It was pretty awful. Sorry, Raney."

I waved it away. "No, you're right. It was terrible. You're not the only ones who thought so." The Rotten Tomatoes score was something like a 2 – not as bad as *Police Academy 4*, say, but bad enough that the studio released it straight to video.

Mrs. Yamamoto was still holding my hand. "You're an undine," she said.

I don't think I hid my surprise very well. "Why, yes. Well, half undine."

She turned to Collum. "And you're a gnome. And you" – her gaze moved to Gail – "are a sylph. Isn't that interesting?" She dropped my hand finally and attached herself to Rufus's elbow. "You must have some friends in high places."

He grinned and looked at his feet. "It's a long story, Auntie."

"You'll have to tell me all about it over dinner," she said.

"Here, sit down," he said, guiding her to a chair. We took that as our cue to find our own seats around the glass-topped patio table. "How are *you* doing? The last I knew, you were supposed to have some kind of surgery."

"Yes," she said. "For skin cancer."

"Oh, no," I said.

"It's fine," she told me. "The surgeon must have gotten it all because it's been five years and it hasn't come back."

"Six years," Annie said, bringing out plates and silverware.

"That's right. It was six years ago. Time flies when you're old." She laughed a little.

Gail half-rose. "Do you need help?" she asked Annie.

"I'd love some. Come on and help me with the drinks," she said, and the two women went into the house.

I thought I should go with them, but Mrs. Yamamoto patted my knee. "You stay," she said. "We have things to discuss."

"We do?" I said.

She nodded. "I know something of the mission the four of you are on."

Rufus leaned forward in his chair. "Do you know where we can find the Fire Key? Or who the guardian is?"

"Any information you have would help us a lot," I said.

"I don't have much," she said. "But I can tell you where you can find out everything you need to know."

"That's awesome!" I said. "Where is this place?"

"It's just outside the national park," she said. "There's a heiau — a shrine to the Hawaiian spirits — where you may find the information you seek."

"You don't mean that one by the Thurston lava tubes?" Annie asked, bringing out a tray laden with tall glasses. "Jasmine iced tea. There's sugar if you want it."

"Sorry, Leprechaun," Rufus said to Collum with a gleam in his eye. "There's no milk for your tea."

"Oh, did you want milk?" Annie asked with a frown. "I can bring some out."

Collum side-eyed Rufus, which sent him off into gales of laughter. "No, I'm fine," Collum assured Annie. "Rufus is in the habit of tickling himself."

"You should have seen your face," Rufus said. The memory set him off again, which made me laugh. Pretty soon all of us were laughing.

Gail handed the glasses around. "That's a first. I've never seen a Salamander giggle before."

"Whew!" Rufus wiped his eyes with the edge of his shirt sleeve. "Okay. I'm fine now. Really." He burbled once or twice more before he completely settled down.

Annie and Gail had begun heading back to the kitchen when Mrs. Yamamoto called after them. "Annie? What about the lava tubes?"

She came partway back. "They're closed. Remember? Because of the eruption."

"But what about the heiau?" Mrs. Yamamoto asked.

"I think the lava got it," Annie said, and turned back toward the house.

"Oh. Oh dear." Mrs. Yamamoto thought for a few moments. "Well, there's another one, but it's farther away. I think that one survived the eruption." She thought again. "Yes, I'm sure it did. You should go tomorrow. I'll have Annie loan you a map."

Dinner was very American – sloppy Joes, baked beans, and potato salad. "You remembered!" Rufus said in delight.

Annie turned a becoming shade of pink. She leaned toward me. "It's his favorite," she said in a stage whisper.

"And here I thought everything he ate was his favorite," I said with a grin.

"Oh haha," Rufus said. He glanced at Mrs. Yamamoto's plate. She was eating slowly, picking her way around her plate, the way old folks do. She caught him looking at her plate and, with a glare, shoved it farther away from him.

Annie shook her finger at him in mock severity. "Don't even think about it, mister. You let Mom eat in peace. There's more in the kitchen if you're still hungry."

He gave her a guilty smile and got up. "Anybody need anything?"

"I need for you to leave some for Mom's lunch tomorrow," Annie said. Then she got up. "Wait. I'll go with you."

"You don't trust me!" he said, clutching his shirt in the middle of his chest.

"You bet I don't," she said. "Not after that one time…"

They bickered companionably as they headed inside. I turned to Annie's mother. "Maybe she should have married Rufus instead of Branson."

Mrs. Yamamoto smiled. "There's time. The world has not stopped turning yet." She glanced at Gail. "Which reminds me – Gail, I have something to show you. Would you join me?"

"Of course," said Gail, puzzled. But she pulled out the older woman's chair and went off with her, into a thicket of tropical plants that bordered the backyard. Pretty soon they'd vanished.

"I wonder what that's all about," Collum said.

I shrugged. "No clue."

Presently Annie and Rufus returned. Rufus's plate was heaped with food, but he was sharing it with her. Collum and I exchanged a wide-eyed look.

"We're missing a few people," Annie said.

"They went that way," I said, pointing. "Mrs. Yamamoto wanted to show Gail something,"

Annie laughed. "Don't call her that. Call her Auntie Helen." She nodded to Collum. "You, too."

"Is that a family custom?" Collum asked.

"Exactly," she said. "A family custom. Isn't that right, Mom?"

Mrs. Yamamoto – okay, fine, Auntie Helen – had emerged from the thicket with Gail right behind her. "What's that?" the older woman called.

"I'm telling them about *ohana*," Annie said. "And why they should call you Auntie."

Auntie Helen nodded as she seated herself at the table again. Then she gave Rufus a sharp look. "Didn't you explain it before you came?"

"Didn't think of it," he said. "Sorry."

Auntie Helen sighed, as if deeply disappointed in him. Then she winked at us and said, "Here in Hawaii, we consider close friends and neighbors to be part of our extended family – our *ohana*. Rufus has been *ohana* since Annie married Branson" – here Annie wrinkled her nose in distaste – "and now you three and Rufus are *ohana*, so we are all *ohana*." She raised her arms in an expansive gesture and nodded decisively, as if that settled it. "Everyone in your age group is your cousin, or brother or sister, and everyone older than you is an auntie or an uncle."

"So the four of us are cousins?" Collum said.

"Oh, no. The four of *you* are brothers and sisters."

I looked at my favorite gnome in mock dismay. "We're in trouble," I said, and everyone laughed.

"It's all right," Auntie Helen assured us. "Old Hawaii was a lot more liberal about that sort of thing than the *haole* have ever been." She dropped us another wink. "But anyway, family members watch out for one another, and help each other whenever the need arises. Oh yes – Annie, get the map. We need to give them directions to Kalalea Heiau."

Chapter 5 – Sunday with little men

Auntie Helen was right about one thing: Kilauea's most recent eruption had totally missed Kalalea Heiau. The lava had flowed east-southeast to the sea. Kalalea was west and south — way south. In fact, the shrine to the old Hawaiian gods was at the southernmost point of the United States.

Auntie Helen told us to get there before sunrise. "The place will be crawling with tourists later on, and you won't find what you're seeking," she'd said. "Don't wear red. And Gail and Raney, you must stay outside the heiau."

"What?" I squeaked.

"Why?" asked Gail in more measured tones.

"It's *kapu*," Auntie Helen said. I knew that word — it's Hawaiian for taboo. She told us women were never allowed in the heiau. The implication was that it was a Hawaiian thing — us *haole* wouldn't understand.

Normally, I might have been a jerk about it and gone in anyway — but not when the future existence of the Earth was at stake. I promised myself that I'd come back someday and go into the shrine, just for spite. Stupid ancient Hawaiian men were stupid.

Assuming the Earth still existed when we were done with this.

Well, it just *would*, that's all. We wouldn't allow ourselves to fail.

We left while it was still dark. The drive took more than an hour, and featured enough hairpin turns and other delights that Collum practically had to pry his hands from the steering wheel when we arrived.

The road leveled out as dawn began to break. We passed a wind farm on our way, the turbines like ghostly sentinels in the half light. Then bad asphalt. Then no asphalt. We parked the rental car at the end of the sort-of-paved part and walked into the stiff breeze the rest of the way to the heiau.

We learned later that the shrine marked the spot where, legend had it, the first Polynesians had landed in Hawaii. To our right was a steep cliff, its edge adorned with wooden contraptions that Google told us were hoists for boats, both to drop them into the water below and to get them out again. Some fishermen had arrived and were beginning to set up their solitary worksites.

To our left was a much gentler slope to the beach. Everywhere was prairie grass – an odd sight in Hawaii – and the unrelenting wind.

The heiau was nothing but a platform of black stone. King Kamehameha II had ordered all the heiaus torn down in the name of progress in 1819, even before the Christian missionaries arrived. Despite that, a sense of sacredness hung around the site at this liminal hour.

Gail and I nodded to the guys and traipsed off to a spot a respectful distance away. Then we turned our backs to the ocean roaring behind us and observed.

The guys, meanwhile, scoped out the original entrance to the heiau. As the sun edged above the waves, they carefully entered the sacred space where that entrance would have been. Rufus went first, with Collum close behind. Both of them faced south and raised their arms in supplication. "Guardians of this place," Rufus intoned, "we ask for your forbearance. We have been charged with protecting the Earth and with keeping it from being destroyed. We are searching for something we believe is in your possession – a Fire Key. Please help us find it. Please help the Earth survive."

Then he and Collum stood there, arms held high. At some prearranged signal, both men dropped to one knee and bowed their heads to the ground.

I briefly debated whether to follow suit, but we weren't part of the ritual, so I didn't. In another minute, I was glad – because if I'd prostrated myself, I wouldn't have seen the five little men who trooped up from the beach.

When I say little men, I don't mean Oompa Loompas, although the thought did cross my mind. These guys were simply short – shorter than Collum, although not as short as a midget would be. Their bodies were proportioned normally and they had the bronzed skin I associated with native Hawaiians. They were shirtless and shoeless, and wore board shorts instead of the grass togas I half-expected them to wear.

The newcomers didn't bother using the traditional entrance – they simply stepped over the remains of the seaside wall. "Who comes to us with tales of Earth's imminent destruction?" the fellow in the middle asked.

For about the millionth time, I wished we'd come up with a team name. Not to mention costumes.

"We are Elementals," Rufus said. "I am a salamander. My companion is a gnome. An ancient evil is loose, and it's gathering up the ancient Keys. We are charged with stopping him."

"That's only two Elements," the man said. "Where are the others?"

Somewhat tentatively, Collum pointed to Gail and me.

"Ah," the man said, and beckoned to us.

We came toward the heiau and stopped. "We were told women weren't allowed," Gail said.

The fellow waved it away. "Times change," he said. "Come on in." So we held our breath – well, I held mine, anyway – and stepped over the wall.

Nothing happened. The little men didn't flee and the Earth neither rocked on her foundations nor opened a crater and swallowed us up. "Stupid ancient Hawaiian men," I muttered.

That got a laugh out of the little men. "We are menehune," the guy in charge said. "I am Hanu, and these are my brothers. We are charged with guarding this heiau. And you are … ?"

"Raney," I said. "I'm an undine. This is Gail – she's a sylph. And you've already met Collum and Rufus." Heads nodded all around.

"This ancient evil you speak of," Hanu said. "Is it a demon?"

"Yes," I said. "And it has my father in thrall."

"I see. And the demon is the one looking for the Fire Key."

"Yes, with my father's help."

Hanu nodded thoughtfully. "We have been watching them," he said.

I started. "You know where they are?"

The little men chuckled. "Oh yes, we know," Hanu said. "And they are not here."

One of the other men said gleefully, "We have been keeping them busy on the north side of the island."

Another guy said, "There are a lot of ruins on the island. A *lot* of ruins."

We all began to laugh. "I like you guys a lot," Rufus said.

Hanu bowed. "We are happy to assist."

"So where's the Key?" Collum asked.

Instantly, the guys' faces drooped. "We cannot tell you," Hanu said. "We guard this heiau, but we do not guard the Key."

"Do you know who does?" Gail asked.

"The answer will be revealed to you when the time is right," said Hanu. "But take heart. The demon will not trouble you while you search for it. We will make sure of that."

"*Lots* of ruins," the third guy said, and grinned.

The four of us exchanged smiles. "Thanks for whatever help you can give us," Rufus said. "We are in your debt."

"No debt is owed to us," Hanu said. "Find the Key and keep it safe. That is all the payment we require." With a final nod, the five little men turned and trooped back down the slope toward the beach.

"Well, that bites," Rufus said when they were gone.

"Yeah," Collum said. "At least we know where not to look."

"We do?" I said.

He nodded. "Yeah. It's not on the north shore, or the menehune wouldn't be keeping Damien busy up there."

"True. That doesn't actually narrow the possibilities all that much, though." I gazed to the east. The sun was nearly up and the ocean sparkled. I sighed.

"Want to swim back?" Rufus asked me mischievously.

"Not particularly – although it's tempting." My eyes strayed south. "The Pacific's a big place. I wonder how far you have to go to hit land again."

"A long, long way," said Gail. "The distances between island chains is so vast out here, it's a wonder the Polynesians found any at all."

"You're not kidding. We still can't find where Amelia Earhart went down," Collum said.

"Come on," said Rufus. "Let's get breakfast. There's a bakery in that town we passed through, and I'm hungry."

Gail laughed. "When *aren't* you hungry?"

As the others began the hike back to the car, I let my eyes linger on the ocean for a moment. Some distance off the coast, I thought I saw a glint of…smoke? Fire, maybe?

But when I looked again, it was gone, and it didn't reappear. I decided it must have been a trick of the morning light.

The food was pretty good at that bakery Rufus had spotted. At last even he was satisfied. He leaned back and stretched. "Well, now what do we do?"

"Go back to the hotel and take a nap," Collum said with a yawn. He tossed the keys to Rufus. "You can drive. I'm not doing that route ever again."

Gail ignored them. She had grabbed a free tourist map of the island from a stand near the door. Now she spread it out on the table before us. "The Key is in or near a volcano, right?"

"Right," I said.

"And there are five active volcanoes on the island." She pointed them out on the map. "Kohala is way up north – the Key can't be there. And I'd bet it's not at Mauna Kea, either. Or Hualalai."

Rufus leaned his forearms on the table. "Is your deduction based on something, or is it just gut feeling?"

"Gut feeling," she admitted. "I could do a flyover of those two, but it would take time. And despite what our new friends said, I don't think we have all that much time. Damien's not stupid. It won't take too many wild goose chases before he realizes he's being played."

"Anyway, isn't Mauna Kea where that big protest is happening?" I asked.

"Protest?" said Collum.

"Yeah. Somebody wants to build a telescope on the summit, and Native Hawaiians have been protesting there to slow down construction." My finger hovered over the spot on the map.

Rufus's face turned a blotchy red. "That volcano is sacred to the Hawaiians. *All* the volcanoes here are." He shook his head. "Some of the idiots pushing this project say it's too late for the locals to complain, since there are already a bunch of telescopes at the summit. Like violating sacred space is okay if it's already been done."

"Getting back to our dilemma," Gail said, with a nod to Rufus's anger, "and given the media attention Mauna Kea is getting right now, it's unlikely that Damien would spend much time looking around there."

Rufus reluctantly agreed. "So what does that leave us?"

Gail pointed to the two remaining volcanoes on the island. "One is Mauna Loa, and the other one is Kilauea, which we've already checked out."

Collum pulled out his pocket computer and signed into the bakery's wifi. After a few minutes of searching, he said, "Mauna Loa's most recent eruption was in the spring of 1984. So it's still considered active. And it's huge." He looked up at Gail. "Lava from previous eruptions has gone all the way to Hilo. Can you cover all that ground in one flyover?"

45

"I'm gonna try," Gail said. "At the very least, we'll be able to knock some more areas off our list." She tossed some cash on the table for her share of the meal. "I'll see you guys back at the hotel," she said, and left.

"Antsy," Rufus commented.

"Can you blame her?" I asked. "All this uncertainty is eating away at me, too."

"Well, I'm ready to head back," said Rufus. "I'd like to get another look at the area around Kilauea. We didn't get anywhere near the most recent flows, where the lava fell into the sea."

"Have a good time," said Collum. "I was serious about the nap. That drive took a lot out of me."

Rufus turned to me. "Raney?"

"Drop me off at Volcano Village," I said. "I'd like to do some shopping."

He barked a laugh. "You're not serious."

"You guys wouldn't let me go in for a soak this morning," I said. "If I can't do that, then retail therapy is the next best thing."

The highway was much less treacherous in daylight. Rufus had us back in an hour or so. He stopped at the hotel first to let Collum out, then dropped me off near the gaggle of cute little artist's studios, shops, and restaurants. "Want me to pick you up on my way back?" he asked.

"Nah. I can walk back from here," I said, and sent him on his way. Then I wandered the streets.

I found some lovely pieces of art that would have looked fabulous in my beach house, but then I remembered: a) I didn't know how soon I'd be home again, and b) I was unemployed. Regretfully, I put everything back.

But then in a jeweler's studio, I found something that fit my budget – an anklet with a tiny sea turtle charm attached. I rarely wore jewelry – it was too easy to lose when I went for a soak – but this little thing seemed perfect. Plus it was a tangible remembrance of the time a sea turtle saved my life.

I mean, that might be a bit overstated. You never know what that golem might have done if it had gotten hold of me, though.

The artist was thrilled. "I loved making that honu. I'm sure you'll give him a good home."

"Honu?"

"Oh, yes. Haven't you heard about the Hawaiian custom of aumakua?" When I shook my head, she said, "Aumakua are family spirits. Sometimes they're gods, but oftentimes a relative will come back after death as a particular animal or plant, so the family sets up a shrine to honor them. In the old days, some families had many aumakua."

"That's lovely," I said, thinking, *lots and lots of ruins on this island.* "What was it that you called this one?"

"It's a honu. A sea turtle. It stands for wisdom and good luck."

"I could use both of those," I said. Then I was seized with an inspiration. "Would you hang onto this for me? I'd like to look around a little more."

"Of course! I'll put it next to the register. Whenever you're ready."

I smiled my thanks and began searching for Elemental aumakua. If we couldn't get t-shirts, we could at least get rings.

I found my ring right away – a sea turtle, of course, in silver. And then I got bogged down. Which animal should I pick for my teammates? Would Gail prefer a hawk or an owl? And what should I get for Collum? There weren't any land mammals among the shop's offerings, and I didn't feel right about picking out a dolphin or something without his input.

I was holding the silver honu ring and mulling over the wisdom of commissioning rings for the rest of the team, given that I was unemployed, when the bell over the door jangled. I half-heard the voices of the newcomers, and was aware of an unpleasant feeling in the air. But what shook me out of my reverie was a familiar and not-at-all-welcome voice calling, "Hey, Raney!"

47

Slowly I turned and came face-to-face with my jerk of an ex-boyfriend.

Inside, I was shrieking with rage, but I managed to keep my expression neutral. "Stone," I said. "I heard you were in town."

"Yeah, we're shooting up in Waipio Valley." He glanced at the sweet young thing who had come into the shop with him. "You know Nyala, don't you?" I did, sort of. She was an up-and-coming actor who'd just been breaking into the business when she appeared on my show. If I'd had a scene with her, I didn't remember it – but I did remember seeing her around the set. We nodded at each other as Stone continued talking about himself. "It sure is beautiful up there. But these volcanoes, am I right? I just can't seem to stay away."

"Yeah," I said, "I heard you were here a few days ago. You must have a lot of down time in the shooting schedule if you have time to drive back here so often. Not shooting many scenes, huh?" I smiled sweetly at him.

He glared at me. "For your information, I'm starring in this film," he said loftily. "The trouble is there's some moron of a developer who keeps getting in our way."

Oh no. It couldn't be. "How's that?" I said, trying not to let my rising panic show.

"He's looking for the perfect location for a new resort, he says. But he wants it to be near some kind of historical shrine or something, and he keeps getting bad information about where this shrine is."

Lots and lots and LOTS of ruins on this island …

"Huh," I said. "Some people get a bad idea in their head and just can't give up on it. Funny how that works." Having sunk that barb, I turned to the artist and put the ring on the counter next to the ankle bracelet. "I'm ready to check out."

He was silent for a solid minute, working out how I'd insulted him. Finally he stomped up to me as I handed my credit card to the artist. "So what are *you* doing in Hawaii? I know you're not *working*. I heard you got bounced from your precious *show*." He addressed his next remark to the artist. "Be careful. She might stiff you."

The card reader chimed, and APPROVED flashed across the tiny screen in big, friendly letters. The artist and I exchanged a smile as she handed over the receipt for me to sign. As I handed it back, I said over my shoulder, "Get lost, Stone."

"Stone," Nyala said in a tiny voice, "let's just go."

He looked at Nyala, glowered at me, and stalked out behind her.

The artist crossed her arms and leaned against the counter. "What a charming fellow."

"Yeah. Dunno what I ever saw in him. Hey, can I get your card? I'm traveling with some friends and we may throw you some business before we leave."

"It's already in the bag," she said. "Thank you for your patronage, Ms. Meadows." She leaned closer. "I love your show. I think they made a big mistake when they let you go."

"Thanks. It was going to be our last season anyway." I picked up my bag and turned to leave.

"Oh, really?" she said. "I heard it got renewed."

I turned back, shock evident on my face. "It did? You heard it recently?"

"A couple of days ago. I'm sorry," she hastened to add.

"It's okay," I said automatically. Then I reached into the bag, found the box with the ring in it, and jammed it on a finger. "Who knows? Maybe it was good luck that I got bounced." I waved to her and left the store.

Then I ran to Annie's Place.

I mean, it was lunchtime anyway. But I really needed a safe spot to sit and process everything I'd just learned. As I pushed open the door, I hoped belatedly that Stone hadn't gotten here first.

Luckily, the place was Stone-free. I took a seat and glanced over the menu distractedly. When the waitress stopped by to take my order, I blurted, "Where's Annie?"

49

"She went home for lunch. What'll you have?"

"I…" I paused. "I'm sorry. I'm a little frazzled." I gave her my order, then stared off into space. When my plate lunch arrived, I ate it without tasting it.

The show had been on the verge of cancellation. Now it had been renewed. Had I been dragging it down? Did my departure breathe new life into a tired formula?

And when I got home, I'd be starting from square one, career-wise. I'd have to find another agent while hoping Sid hadn't poisoned the waters against me. Would I ever get another acting job in Hollywood? I mean, I'd been thinking of going into directing – I'd done a little bit of it already, and lots of actors ended up liking it better behind the camera than in front of it – but could I even get hired doing that? Right now, I was considered a flake. Directors couldn't be flakes. Neither could actors, but it was easier for them to get away with it. At least for a while.

Except I wasn't a flake. I had a perfectly good explanation for those photos of me with a twenty-foot-tall land wight. Just none that any sane person in Hollywood would believe.

Not that there were many sane people in Hollywood. After all, somebody had renewed *Story of a Homicide*. Had I been dragging the show down?

Round and round my thoughts went.

Somewhere in the maelstrom, I put on my new ankle bracelet. I fancied I felt a little jolt of power as the sea turtle on my ankle connected with the one on my finger.

Then I paid the bill – studiously avoiding Stone's photo on the wall – and headed over to Annie's house.

I expected Annie to answer my knock on the door, but it was Mrs. Yamamoto – sorry, Auntie Helen – who pulled it open. "Oh good," she said. "You're here. We've been waiting for you."

I blinked. "We?" Then I felt something winding around my ankles and looked down. "Tiger!" I cried. "How did you get here?"

The portly orange tabby ignored my question. Instead, she said, *I like Annie and Auntie Helen. They gave me albacore.*

Chapter 6 – Sunday with Auntie Helen and friends

Gail was there, too. She was in the backyard, deep in conversation with Annie over jasmine iced tea, and she looked troubled.

Her expression shifted when she saw me: first surprised, then guilty, then carefully bland. *Guilty? What's that about, I wonder?*

"I see you found the cat," she said, indicating the troublesome critter in my arms.

"I thought maybe it was the other way around." I skritched Tiger under her chin a few more times, then put her down – she was too heavy to hold for very long. Her globe-trotting ways obviously hadn't affected her appetite.

"No," Gail said, "she was here when I got here. And she's not speaking to me again." She looked miffed.

I made a mental note to chat with the cat about that later. Aloud, I said to her, "So you just showed up here? How did you know where to find us?"

I told you before – I know how you smell. She waddled over to a plumeria tree, sniffed at a cluster of flowers on a low-hanging branch, and sneezed.

"Okay, but you couldn't have followed your nose here because I wasn't here when you got here." Then I winced. "Did that sound as weird to you as it did to me?"

Annie laughed. "Have a seat. I'll get you some iced tea."

"That would be lovely," I said gratefully, and sank into a chair.

"Have you eaten?" she called.

"Yeah, I stopped in at your restaurant and had the plate lunch. Although I was really kind of looking for a place to hide."

"Oh?" She brought out the glass and set it before me, then resumed her seat. "You do look a little bit spooked."

I barked a laugh. "You could say that. I ran into an ex-boyfriend in a jewelry shop."

"Oh, your ring! Is it new?" She leaned across the table to examine it. I willingly relinquished my hand to her.

"Yeah, I got it this morning. And an ankle bracelet that kind of matches." I kicked my leg up above the level of the table, grateful that I was wearing shorts and not a skirt.

"Very cute," she said. "I guess the sea turtle spoke to you."

"You could say that," Gail said dryly as she sipped her tea.

"There was an incident on Waikiki," I said, and explained the whole thing to Annie and her mother. When I was finished, the two of them traded looks of concern.

Auntie Helen spoke first. "It sounds to me like *honu* has chosen you. It's good of you to honor him in this way." She nodded toward Gail. "Your sister has an aumakua, too."

"Really?" I said. "Owl or hawk?"

She looked at me strangely. "Hawk. It's called an *io* here." She looked to Annie, who nodded. "I had one lead me around when I did the flyover just now."

"Like you asked it for help? Or it volunteered?"

"Volunteered. It was an odd feeling. I'm not used to animals being sentient."

"I'm not either, actually. It all started for me when I met Tiger." I glanced at the cat, who was now snoozing in the sunshine next to the plumeria. "So did you see anything useful?"

"That's the weirdest part," said Gail. "I was mainly tracking Mauna Loa's rift zones, thinking that if I could see where the most recent lava flows have gone, I could eliminate those areas from our search, since the marker for the Key would be buried. But then the hawk showed up and had me veer off-course."

"Where did it take you?"

"South Point."

I frowned. "That's where we were this morning."

"I know."

"Huh. That *is* weird." I pondered it for a moment. "I mean, there's a heiau there. Is that the marker?" I looked at Auntie Helen, who shrugged. I turned back to Gail. "I sure wish we knew who the guardians were. This would be a lot easier if we could just talk to them."

"No kidding," said Gail. "We don't even know what the Key looks like."

Annie sat up straighter. "You don't know?"

"We never saw either of the other Keys," I explained. "We know the Earth Key was small enough to fit in a cask of bog butter, and we saw the cask, but we never saw the Key itself. And Damien grabbed the Water Key before we even knew all of this stuff existed." I tapped the glass tabletop. "We've been flying blind this whole time."

"Wait just a minute," Auntie Helen said, rising from her chair with an effort and heading inside.

We made a half-hearted attempt at chitchat, but the conversation died when Auntie Helen returned, lugging a book covered in tattered, rotting leather. "I am not the guardian," she said as she sat again. "But the old guardians gave me this as a gift many years ago." Carefully, she turned the crumbling pages. "There. Those are the Keys."

Gail and I jumped up and ran to Auntie's side. I pulled out my phone and took photos of the page for future reference.

The Keys didn't look like keys at all. Or at least not the things I think of as keys, with a finger-grip attached to a longish jagged piece.

The Water Key was shaped like a cresting wave with a prominent hook at the top. The Fire Key looked like tongues of flame, several of which seemed to bend over or inward. The Air Key resembled a tornado with its conical shape. The Earth Key looked like a rock.

"Just like a gnome," I muttered. "No imagination."

"Or no time," Gail said with a grin. "I suspect that when you're trying to lock up a thing that has the power to destroy the Earth, artistry is the least of your worries. You just want to make sure the lock will work. And that it will survive the ages."

Auntie turned the page and I gasped. The illustration here was of a beach – water on the left, then sand, then huge boulders, and sea grass and low shrubs up a rise on the right. The vegetation was on fire, though, and a waterspout hovered nearby. And in the middle was what I could only describe as a mouth of hell. Flames licked the edges of the portal, and nothing of the other side could be seen.

"That doesn't look like a Hawaiian beach," I said.

"It's not," said Auntie. "It's somewhere in North America."

"Look familiar?" asked Gail.

I shook my head. "Not really, no. I mean, California has rocky beaches, but so does Oregon. And New England."

"I wondered because of what Niall said."

After Surgat had swiped the Earth Key from the cellar under the Barths' thatched cottage, Collum's mother had basically forced his father to tell us what he knew. Niall was the one who told us the Fire Key was here in Hawaii. When I'd asked him if he knew where the door was –the one with the locks that all these Keys were fashioned for – he gave me a weird look and basically said I ought to know already. Which I didn't. If I had, would I have bothered asking?

I shook my head. "It's not ringing a bell. Sorry. I wish I knew why he said that to me."

"Did you get your picture?" Auntie Helen asked, peering up at me.

I'd been too shocked by the illustration. I grabbed the photo now. "Anything else in there that might be of use to us?"

She slid the volume toward me. "Feel free to take pictures of every page, if you want." So I did, starting with the pages she'd skipped past and going on to the very end of the book. I clicked through as quickly as possible, while still taking care not to damage the fragile pages. It took a fair amount of concentration, so I was only half-listening to the conversation when it resumed. I did, however, hear Annie say softly, "Are you gonna tell them?"

And I heard Gail's response, just as soft: "Not yet."

Presently Gail took her leave. Annie saw her to the front door. When they were gone, I looked at Auntie Helen and said, "What's up with Gail?"

"She is working through some things," she responded. "Your task has brought up some uncomfortable memories. We were discussing them when you arrived."

"So counseling, huh?" I said with a smile. "Want to have a whack at me?"

That sent her off into gales of laughter. "Oh, Raney," she said, "no one is more transparent than you. Your feelings are right there on your face for all the world to see."

I thought about my meetup with the ex earlier in the day. "I hope you're right. Because then the ex will never stick his nose in my business, ever again."

"I'm sure he got the message," she said.

"Yeah, but will he honor it? The guy's a narcissist and a sociopath. If he can give me trouble, he will – it won't matter how I feel about it. In fact, if it upsets me or causes me pain, he's sure to do it." Then I stopped. "Oh. Oh, no."

"What is it?" Annie asked as she returned.

I sucked in a breath. "So the ex I saw at the jewelry store was Stone." I hated that I had to say his name. I still didn't want to give him any notoriety, even if it was just in my head. "He told me their production schedule kept getting delayed because some rich developer kept insisting he had to investigate the place where they were shooting."

Annie's eyebrows shot up. "You think it's your father?"

"Yeah," I said. "Yeah, I do. And if Stone realizes what's going on with us – if he mentions seeing me to someone connected with my father and *he* realizes we're over here, looking for the Key…" I took a photo of the last page in the book and closed it gently. "I need to get back to the hotel and tell the others."

"I'll give you a ride," Annie said.

Chapter 7 – still Sunday, now with aumakua

Tiger insisted on coming along, even after I told her the hotel wouldn't let her in. *Nice try, sister,* she said as she jumped into the back seat of Annie's SUV. I felt a little guilty as I watched her triangulate the distance against her body weight. I mean, I could have picked her up and put her in the car, but I was annoyed with her for following us *again.* If she could travel halfway around the world to find us, she was more than capable of getting into a car under her own power.

In the end, she managed it fine. Then I wondered whether the struggle had been for show, and was annoyed with her all over again. Once I was buckled in, I half-turned in my seat and glared at her. "Why have you stopped speaking to Gail *this* time?" I demanded.

Don't trust her anymore.

"Could you be more specific?" I said acidly.

No.

"Because we've already had this discussion, missy, and I made myself quite clear then that… Are you seriously going to take a nap while I'm talking to you?" Because she'd curled up in a ball on the back seat. "You are *so* not going to ignore me!" I reached between the seats and grabbed her tail.

She lashed her tail furiously, pulling it out of my grasp, and hissed at me.

"Tiger!" I was shocked. And hurt. Not physically hurt, but heart hurt.

She turned a gimlet eye on me. *Do not lay your hands upon me in anger, human.*

"Fine. I'm sorry."

Hmph. She put her head back down and closed her eyes again, but I knew she wasn't asleep – the tip of her tail still twitched.

I sighed and faced forward again. "I guess I'll find out in due time."

"I'm sure you will," Annie said. I looked at her just in time to see the same fleeting look of guilt I'd seen on Gail's face. Then she concentrated on her driving.

We had only gone a mile or so before we overtook Gail trudging along on the opposite shoulder. Annie pulled up next to her and rolled her window down. "Want a lift?" she called.

"I remembered something," I called. "It's important."

She sighed and climbed in the back. Tiger saw her coming and sprang between the seats, then curled up at my feet. Gail rolled her eyes and, with another sigh, buckled herself in.

"Sorry for imposing our dysfunctional family on you," I said to Annie.

She bestowed on me a sunny smile. "It's no trouble at all. Really." She hit the gas. "Besides, this way I get to see Rufus."

I shot her a sidelong glance. "You really like him, don't you?" She didn't need to answer – her reddened cheeks did the talking for her. So I asked, "Then why did you marry his cousin?"

"It's a long story. Rufus seemed a little too crazy. Bran seemed steadier by comparison."

"You weren't wrong about Rufus," I said.

"Oh, he's mellowed a lot."

My eyes widened. "He *has?*"

She laughed. "Trust me. He was *really* crazy when he was younger."

I'd once watched him slag a guy's cellphone with the heat of one hand. I shook my head. "The mind boggles."

Gail practically flew out of the car. "Gotta freshen up," she said. "I'll meet you guys at the overlook in back."

I left the door open so Cranky Kitty could jump down. She landed with a little kitty *oof*, then preceded us to the hotel entrance. "They may not let you in unaccompanied," I called.

She stopped and sat, giving us her inscrutable look. Annie scooped her up and strode on ahead. "She's my emotional support cat," I heard her tell the bellhop.

As I passed the mystified guy, I offered by way of explanation, "A cat fits better under an airline seat than a peacock." Then I scooted ahead of my companions and pointed down the hallway to the left. "It's this way."

Collum was up and in the bathroom when I let myself into our room. "Are you decent?" I called.

"Depends on the activity you had in mind," he responded.

I couldn't help but grin. "We'll discuss that later. I had an adventure in town that I need to tell you guys about. Annie gave me a ride back. Can she come in?"

"Yeah, sure." He emerged from the bathroom, shirtless and freshly showered, and reached for a t-shirt laying on the bed.

"Hang on," I said, stepping up to him. "I need a piece of that before you put it away." I wrapped my arms around him and rubbed my cheek on his bare chest. "Mmmm. Okay, I'm good now."

He chuckled and kissed me. Then he began pulling on his shirt.

I walked back to the door, calling over my shoulder, "Tiger's here."

His head popped out from the neck of the t-shirt, his expression incredulous. "What?"

I opened the door. "Come on in."

Tiger jumped down from Annie's arms and, without acknowledging Collum, sauntered into the bathroom. *Where's the litter box?*

"We don't have one," Collum said evenly. "We didn't expect you to join us."

Humans. Where am I supposed to pee?

"Outside," he said, one eyebrow raised.

"Where we're all going in a minute," I interjected.

60

"Hi, Annie," said Collum. "Has this ungrateful ball of fur inflicted herself on you?"

She laughed. "Why are you all so hard on her? She's a very sweet cat."

Collum and I exchanged a look. "Right," we said in unison. Then I said, "Gail's meeting us at the caldera overlook out back. Have you seen Rufus?"

"Not since this morning. You ladies go on ahead – I'll roust him out of his room."

"Sounds good," I said. Annie, Tiger, and I went back into the hallway and made for the side door.

"Who does Tiger belong to?" Annie asked.

"Originally, she was Collum's brother's cat," I explained. "After he was killed, Collum tried to move her in with him. But she's sort of attached herself to me."

Could you hurry it up? I have to peeeeee. The last part came out came out as a yowl.

"Keep your shirt on," I said. "And be quiet or you'll get us kicked out. There may be hotel guests who are allergic to cats." I pushed open the door and she raced to the nearest patch of dirt, where she crouched for quite some time.

Collum joined us. "She's not pooping, is she? I don't have anything to clean it up with."

Tiger glared at us. *Do I watch you while you pee?* she asked tartly.

A smile spread slowly across Collum's face. "Actually, yeah, you do," he said.

"Did you find Rufus?" I asked him.

"Nope. But I left him a note to join us out back." And he preceded us around the corner of the building. On our left, a railing was all that separated us from the caldera. On our right, we could see into the ground-level rooms. Many had the blinds drawn, but Rufus's were wide open – the better to view the volcano any time, day or night, I supposed. Collum leaned forward and cupped his hands between his face and the window. "He is definitely not in there," he pronounced.

"He'll join us," Annie said. "I'm sure of it."

Collum dropped his hands and kept moving, and the rest of us followed him.

I wondered briefly why we were letting Annie in on this discussion. This was supposed to be a team meeting, and while it was nice of her to give me a ride and all, she wasn't part of the team. But nobody seemed bothered by the idea except me – not Collum and not Tiger, who wasn't technically part of the team, either, but good luck getting her to leave.

The sidewalk widened and then ended at a patio. Here, you could enter the lobby through a door, or keep going to another walkway dead ahead. Hotel guests sat in comfy chairs next to occasional tables here and there. A few picnic tables sat closer to the rim.

Gail was perched backwards, facing us, on the bench of the picnic table farthest away. She waved us over and swiveled, lifting her legs over the bench, to face the crater. Annie sat next to her, and Collum and I took the bench on the opposite side.

"Rufus?" Gail asked.

"Wasn't in his room," Collum said. "I left him a note."

"I'm sure he'll be along," Annie said.

Gail scowled. "He'd better get here soon. I don't want to have to repeat this."

"I don't, either," I said.

Annie was gazing out over the caldera, looking puzzled. "That's crazy," she murmured.

"What is?" I asked.

"It looks like there's someone out there."

Now I heard the rising tide of conversation around us, as people began to stand and gawk. Someone ran inside in a panic. Collum and I shared an *oh shit* look and turned as one.

Sure enough, here came our Madman, strolling across the smoking crater. His shoes were smoking, too, and he appeared to have something perched on one shoulder.

"I told him not to do that," Gail muttered, exasperated. "The trails were closed for a reason." She got up and hustled to the railing, yelling at him, "What do you think you're *doing*, Rufus?"

Rufus waved. "Hey, guys! I made a friend!"

"Splendid," I muttered.

"I'll be there in a minute," he called, and began climbing up the side of the caldera.

Just then, rangers burst through the door to the lobby, carrying a flat board with handholds – the kind EMTs use when someone may have broken their neck while skiing – and a huge tote with a big red cross on the side. They made a beeline for a locked gate near where we were sitting. People gasped and moved out of their way.

"Guys?" Collum called. "That's not going to be necessary." But the rescue personnel ignored him. A moment more and I heard the sound of a helicopter approaching.

"Oh, boy," I said in dismay.

The rangers got the gate open and headed down the path at a fast trot. At virtually the same time, Rufus's head poked up above the concrete on the other side of the patio. He used the crossbars on the railing to hoist himself up the last few feet, then straight-armed the top rail and did sort of a vault dismount.

Annie was entranced.

"Hey, guys," Rufus repeated, making his way to us. His hands were covered in ash and his shoes were still smoking. "Whoa," he said, spying the open gate. "There's a path? I wish I'd known about that. It would have made getting up here a lot easier."

"Not only that, but you would have met the EMTs that just went down it," said Collum.

"Is that a helicopter?" Rufus said. Then daylight dawned. "Oh. Uh, this isn't for me, is it?"

Gail looked like she was about three seconds away from blowing her top. "I. Told. You."

"I know, I know. But I needed to complete the circle," he said. "Oh, hey, Annie. Nice to see you again."

The EMTs came back through the gate at nearly the same rate they went through it – for which they got big props from me, considering how steep that path was. They took one look at Rufus and stopped dead. "You," the lead ranger said.

"Hey," said Rufus. "Look, I'm really sorry, but this is all a misunderstanding. I was just out hiking."

"We had a report of someone crossing the crater," the ranger said. "Was that you?"

Rufus waved that away. "No way! I was on the trail. Only a madman would walk across the crater, am I right?"

"But all the trails are closed," a man said.

"I saw you climb out," a woman said, pointing to the spot where Rufus did his dismount. "Right over there."

Someone else said, "We all saw you down there. You waved to your friends."

"His shoes are smoking!" a little kid cried.

"He's not wrong," Collum said in an aside to me.

"But I'm fine," Rufus insisted. "Really. See?" He held up both ashy arms. The critter that had been on his shoulder – which I could see now was a lizard – climbed up onto his head.

"We should take his vitals, at least," one of the rangers said. She knelt and pulled a blood pressure cuff from the tote.

"But I'm fi—" Rufus's protestation was cut off by the EMT shoving a temperature probe under his tongue.

"Close your mouth," she said. "And don't open it again until I tell you to, or we'll have to do it over."

64

He threw us a pleading look as the woman yanked up his t-shirt sleeve and slapped the blood pressure cuff around his bicep. But there wasn't a whole lot we could do. It's not like she was hurting him. And if we made too much of a fuss, we might get charged for the call. I was pretty sure the air ambulance service wouldn't come cheap.

The head of the group approached us. "Are any of you related to this man?"

"I'm his cousin," Annie said. Then she turned on the charm. "Hey, you look familiar. Did we go to school together? Volcano Elementary School?"

"Uh, well, yeah, I did."

"I thought so! You were a couple of years ahead of me, though. Right?" Her eyes dropped briefly to his name tag. "Gene Simmons?"

"Gene was my brother. I'm Tom."

"Oh, right! Gene was already in high school then. I'm Annie Yamamoto."

He thought for a second. "Oh, you own Annie's Place! Great food. And we really appreciate the ranger discount."

"Aww," she said, palms out. "Nothing's too good for my NPS buddies. So listen, about my cousin here..."

He leaned in. "Is he a little...?" His index finger made a twirly motion beside his temple. "You know?"

She leaned in closer. "I wouldn't say he's crazy. But sometimes he has spells where he thinks he's some kind of magic guy." She laughed as if she were sharing an in-joke with the ranger. "It's been a real challenge for his parents, let me tell you."

"I'll bet."

"I know they'd really appreciate it if you guys just forgot this ever happened." She turned on a thousand-watt smile.

Ranger Simmons – Tom, not Gene – hesitated for a second. I mean, he had to know he was being played. He looked over at the EMT, who was stowing the blood pressure cuff. "How's our patient?"

65

She shrugged. "He checks out. Vitals good, lungs sound good, no burns, no other apparent injuries. He's gonna need new shoes, but other than that he seems fine."

"Okay." Ranger Simmons all but shrugged. "Must have been a mistake. Pack up and head out." He turned back to Annie and tipped his ranger hat. "Sorry for the inconvenience, folks." And off he went, following his crew.

Rufus walked over to us, pausing every couple of steps to look at the bottoms of his sneakers. "I guess they kind of melted," he said sheepishly. "Thanks, Annie."

I shook my head in wonder at her acting acumen. "If you ever decide to give up the restaurant business, I guarantee I can get you a job in Hollywood," I said.

"I'm just glad you're okay," she said to Rufus. Then, simultaneously, she hugged him and whacked him on the back. "But don't ever scare me like that again."

"Yes, ma'am," he said, returning the hug. Then his hands sprang away from her, leaving gray prints behind. "Uh. Does volcanic grit wash out?"

I looked around. The other guests were still staring at us. One little kid came up to Rufus and poked his leg. "Whoa," he said, and ran off to report back to his buddies.

"Let's reconvene somewhere else," Collum suggested.

"We can go back to my house," Annie said.

"Sounds like a plan," said. Heads down, we strode through the door to the lobby, then through it and out the other side to the parking lot. I felt like a rock star. We needed handlers – people to open doors for us and hold back our legions of screaming fans.

Okay, I made up the screaming fans. I did feel like we were celebrities, though.

Annie jumped into her SUV and fired it up, and we climbed in after her – all but Collum, who followed in our rental. At the last second, Tiger came at a run and vaulted into my lap, sinking her claws into my thighs to help her stop.

"Ow!" I said. "We need to trim your claws."

No!

"Yeah, we do," I said. "You drew blood, I'm sure of it."

But Tiger's attention had been snared by the lizard still perched in the thicket of Rufus's hair. While Annie pulled the car around and turned onto the highway, lizard and cat engaged in a staring contest.

"Don't even think about it," said Rufus to the cat.

CHAPTER 8 – STILL SUNDAY

The lizard stayed in place all the way to Annie's backyard. She looked down a hallway, presumably to the bedrooms, and said in a stage whisper, "Mom's taking a nap." Then she ushered us out to the backyard.

At last, we got to take a breath and compare notes. Rufus gave a more-or-less believable story about his adventure in the caldera of an active volcano. He'd decided to take one more walk around the crater to make sure he hadn't missed anything in the way of a marker, when his new buddy fell out of a tree and onto him. The little fellow made it clear somehow – Rufus couldn't say exactly how, but somehow – that there was nothing here to find, that this was the wrong volcano entirely, and that he needed to head back to the hotel.

"Did you say Kilauea is the wrong volcano?" Gail said.

"That's what this guy tells me," Rufus said.

"I think I've seen that guy," said Collum. "He sells car insurance. But I thought he was Australian."

"He's a gecko," Annie said. "In Hawaiian, he'd be called *mo'o*, which is also the word for dragon."

"He does look kind of prehistoric," I said, admiring his bright green skin and orange spots. "Can I pet him?"

"The reason I'm asking," Gail began, raising her voice.

"Later," Rufus said quietly, and I nodded. We turned our full attention to Gail.

She glared at us as she said, "The reason I'm asking is because I had a similar visitation from a hawk today." And then, relaxing a tiny bit, she told the guys about flying over Mauna Loa, and about the hawk who led her back to Kalalea Heiau. We'd been to the shrine just that morning, but it felt like it had happened days ago. Or even in another lifetime.

"So if Mauna Loa isn't the right volcano, and Kilauea isn't the right volcano, and we'd already knocked the ones farther north off the list…" Gail said.

"Oh, right," I said. "That reminds me. I know where Damien's been."

The gang leaned forward. "Where?" Collum demanded.

"Remember how the menehune said they were keeping him busy up north, looking for ruins of ancient shrines?" The guys nodded. "Well, I ran into an ex-boyfriend in Volcano Village today."

"Is this the same guy…?" Collum's question hung in the air.

"Yeah, it is." I swallowed before going on. "Anyway, he said their production is way behind schedule because there's this rich developer who keeps interrupting them, saying he needs to search for something right where they're supposed to be filming that day."

Everybody got quiet for a minute. Then Collum said, "Damien must be wondering where we are by now."

"And he's going to be in a crappy mood, since none of his searches have panned out," Rufus said.

Nobody needed to fill in the blank aloud: We were running out of time. As soon as Damien found out where we were, he'd be all over us. We needed to figure out where that Key was. Now.

"If it's not Mauna Loa and it's not Kilauea, we've run out of volcanoes," Gail said.

"And if Kalalea is the marker, then we've *really* run out of volcanoes." I glanced at Annie, whose eyes had grown enormous. "Haven't we?"

In a quiet voice, she said, "It's Loihi."

"What?" said Rufus.

"What's Loihi?" asked Collum at the same time.

"It's gotta be," she said, frowning in concentration. "That's the only thing that fits."

"*Annie*," I said. "What is Loihi?"

She focused on me. "It's the youngest volcano in the Hawaiian chain." Seeing blank looks on everyone's faces but Collum's, she said, "Okay. All

69

of the islands in our archipelago were formed by volcanic activity. But unlike a lot of volcanoes – for instance, Mount St. Helens – our volcanoes don't occur along the edge where two tectonic plates come together. Instead, volcanoes here are created when magma rises to a spot somewhere in the middle of a plate and pushes through it. The place where the magma boils through is called a hot spot. With me so far?" Heads nodded all around.

"Okay. So the thing about tectonic plates is that they're always moving. But the hot spot under the plate is stationary. It's kind of like a really long griddle sliding over a stove burner. Every so often, the burner will heat up and cook a pancake that's sitting on top of it. But the next time the burner heats up, a different part of the griddle will be on top of it, so a different pancake will cook.

"The Pacific Plate has been moving northwest for a long, long time, which makes the islands in the northwest part of Hawaii the oldest. The plate has moved so far northwest now that the hot spot has created a new pot of magma under the sea, off the southeast coast of the Big Island. That magma pot has been named Loihi."

"So it's a baby volcano?" I asked.

"Depends on how you define 'baby'. It first began erupting four hundred thousand years ago."

"Wow," I said.

"And it's already ten-thousand feet tall, measured from the sea floor. That's taller than Mount St. Helens was when it erupted in 1980."

"But it's all underwater right now," Collum said.

"Right. The experts say it'll take another ten-thousand years, or maybe as many as a hundred thousand years, before it will begin to poke up above the waves.. It's hard to say. Volcanoes have a mind of their own."

"I guess so," I said.

"So wait," said Gail. "If this new volcano is underwater, how could anyone get there to drop off the Key?"

"Submarine?" Rufus ventured, looking at me. "Or maybe they tied it to a fish."

"Or some other Water creature that can go that deep," I said. "There are all sorts of ways."

"And it's not like it's erupting constantly," said Annie. "Loihi's last eruption was in 1996."

"Could you go down that low?" Collum asked me.

I shrugged. "Maybe. If I knew where to look. We'd need some way to narrow our search area that didn't involve aerial reconnaissance."

Annie tapped the table with her fingernails for a moment. "Be right back," she said, and left us.

I took the opportunity, before anyone objected, to stand up and pet the head of Rufus's gecko. The little guy closed his eyes and seemed to enjoy it. "Have you named him?"

"Moe seemed appropriate," Rufus said.

"Cute," I said, and sat back down – right on top of Tiger, who squalled like a baby. "Oh, stop," I told him as I picked her up and settled her on my lap. "You'll wake up Auntie Helen." I petted her, scratching her in all her favorite spots, and soon had her purring again.

"Maybe she's jealous of the gecko," Gail said with a smile.

I would never be jealous of a lizard. I moved because your seat was warm.

I chuckled. "Have it your way."

"Here it is," Annie said as she rejoined us, carrying a laptop. She set it on the table and turned it so we could see the nifty undersea photography on the screen. "More than four thousand earthquakes were recorded near Loihi during the summer of 1996. The activity caused part of the summit, called Pele's Vents, to collapse. Now the area is known as Pele's Pit." She looked at me. "It's about three thousand feet below the surface. Can you get that far down?"

"I've never tried it, but I don't see why I couldn't. Once I'm disassembled, I'm basically part of the water."

"Could you get the bends, going that low?" Collum asked. I could tell the idea made him queasy. To be honest, it made me a little queasy, too."

"I don't know," I said. "If I remember right, the bends happen when nitrogen builds up in the blood under the pressure of the water. Or something like that. I wouldn't actually have blood circulating, per se, so that may not be a problem for me.

"But there is a practical problem: when I'm one with Water, I can't carry anything. Even if I could find the Key, I'd have no way of bringing it back."

"Not to mention the gas from those vents may be too hot for you to handle," Rufus said. "No matter what state you're in – flesh-and-blood or liquid. If the vents are too hot, you could conceivably boil away."

"Thank you for that comforting mental picture," I said. "Although to be honest, I'd thought of it already."

"So assuming the Key is down there," Gail said, "we have no way to retrieve it."

I tapped my chin with a forefinger. "How deep can sea turtles swim?"

Annie smiled. "About three thousand feet. You might be onto something, Raney."

"Good to hear. Of course, we still have to recruit one."

We chatted for another twenty minutes or so, kicking around ideas, but without making much progress. Pretty soon Auntie Helen woke up and Annie made dinner for all of us.

Eventually, though, we needed to go back to the hotel. "I'm sure the coast is clear by now," Rufus said after dinner. "And we should let you get back to your evening."

"It's no imposition," said Auntie Helen. "After all, you're family."

Rufus and Annie exchanged shy smiles. Which was kind of adorable and also kind of sickening.

"I'll warm up the car," Collum said. "Come on, Raney."

"Right," I said, and followed him. Gail was close on my heels.

So was Auntie Helen. "We'll just give the young people their moment," she said, smiling contentedly.

"Why, it's almost like you planned this," I said with a grin.

"Let's just say I know how to capitalize on an opportunity." She winked. "Annie's been in love with that crazy *haole* for years. Now he's here, out of the blue and – well. I just want to see her happy."

Presently, the "young people" in question came out the front door, hand in hand. I shot Auntie Helen a thumbs-up as the four of us got in the rental car. She and Annie waved until we turned the corner.

When we got back to the hotel, Rufus said, "Anyone for a nightcap?"

"I'm in," said Collum. "Hey, your buddy's gone."

"He jumped down when we got out of the car. I'm sure he'll be back."

We were Tigerless, too. She'd stayed behind with Auntie Helen. She had let me know in no uncertain terms that their backyard was a much better litter box than her options here at the hotel. I reminded her that Collum had said as much when she turned up. In response, she stared at me for a full ten seconds, and then turned her back on me.

We cadged glassware from our respective rooms, and Rufus produced a bottle of Irish whiskey that made Collum whistle and hold out his glass. The four of us got pleasantly sloshed, chatting about this and that.

Eventually the festivities began to wind down. Gail, in particular, was becoming quieter and quieter. I thought about her counseling session with Auntie Helen, and about how we were supposed to be there for one another. So when the guys finally ran out of stuff to talk about, I said to Gail, "It's now or never."

She gave me an innocent look. I gave her a *you know what I mean* look. We locked gazes for a moment. Then she sat forward and waved her glass at the whiskey bottle. "I'll need another round to tell this story," she said, and Rufus obliged. She sipped, let out a sigh of appreciation, and said, "I didn't so much retire from the spook business as they let me go."

"Why?" Rufus asked.

"I fucked up a job. I fucked it up badly enough that we almost went to war over it." She drained her glass and held it out again. Again, Rufus filled it for her.

"I can't give you any details. It's all top secret, need-to-know stuff, even now. It might never be declassified." She took another sip. "But I can tell you that I made a major misstep – I believed someone I shouldn't have believed, and passed along a story that I should have kept to myself." She sat back and swirled the amber liquid in her glass. "I was reprimanded and given a desk job while the bureau conducted a formal inquiry. Being demoted to a desk job is humiliating by itself, although most agents get their names cleared before long. But…" She slouched in her chair. "My confidence was gone. Spying is really a young person's job. Oh, when you first start, you don't know anything and you make a lot of dumb mistakes. But pretty soon you figure out what's what. And then you get smart. You get so you can figure out a target's psychological profile after surveilling him for just ten minutes. Once you have that, you can predict what he'll do next – and about ninety-five percent of the time you'll be right. Except I was right ninety-eight percent of the time. I was the best, I'm telling you. I have a whole wall full of awards at home.

"But then I made this colossal mistake and I began to wonder. I knew I wasn't as quick anymore, or as flexible. My eyesight was starting to go. For the first time in my life, I needed contacts."

"You were getting older," I said.

"Sure. But it seemed like my judgment was going, too. What if it was early Alzheimer's? No way the agency would keep me on if I were losing my mind."

"So you retired," I said.

"And it didn't help." She laughed bitterly. "You know that thing they say? 'Wherever you go, there you are'? Well, it's true. I couldn't escape my mortality by retiring – it came with me." She sat forward as she took another swallow. "And then," she said, "*this* thing came along." Her gesture encompassed all four of us. "And I thought, hey, here's an opportunity to do good again. To *be* someone again. Someone important. Someone special. A mover and shaker." She slumped in the chair. "And then that damned hawk pulled me off-course."

"That damned hawk did us a favor," Rufus said, forehead creased in a frown. "We'd still be looking for the Key in the wrong place."

"Yeah, but it was my idea to look there," Gail said. "Don't you see? I was wrong. *Again.*" She drained her glass and let her hand droop. "And the next Key after this one is the Air Key. *My* Key. What if I'm wrong *again*? What if Damien collects all the Keys and we can't stop him because of some stupid thing I do, and the Earth is destroyed and it's all my fault?" Her face was a mask of self-loathing.

"It might be my fault," Collum said quietly.

"Or mine," I said.

"Or mine," Rufus said. "You don't have a lock on the world's supply of stupidity, Gail."

She looked up at him with a sullen expression.

"Which of us walked through an active volcano today, and ruined his best running shoes?"

A corner of her mouth turned up. "I will give you that one. I've done a lot of dumb things in my life, but I've never done *that*."

"See? There's always somebody dumber than you." He grinned.

"And you've been right about a lot of things," I said. "You were right that I could turn myself into a cloud. I never would have thought to try that on my own."

"And your reconnaissance runs have been invaluable," Collum said. "None of us can do what you do."

She sat quietly for a moment. At last, she gave us a smile. "Okay, you've convinced me. I won't throw myself into the caldera tonight."

I blinked. "You weren't seriously considering it, were you?"

"Not after I got a look at his shoes," she said, hooking a thumb at Rufus. Then she stood. "I'm going to get some shut-eye. But seriously, gang, thanks." She looked at each of us in turn. "I worked alone for so long that I forgot what it's like to be part of a team. You guys are…" She looked into her empty glass. "I'm going right now, before I start bawling in front of everybody."

I got up and gave her a hug, whispering, "There's nothing wrong with crying. Tears always help *me*."

She nodded and hugged me briefly. "Thanks, Raney. Well, goodnight."

As the door closed behind her, Collum stood. "We should head for bed, too. Let's meet up for breakfast around ten, maybe?"

"That'll be second breakfast for me, but okay," Rufus said.

"Sweet dreams, Rufus," I said. Then, feeling mischievous, I added, "I bet Annie will dream about you tonight."

He shook his head. "You're as bad as Auntie Helen. Get out of my room."

Not long afterward, lying beside Collum in the dark, I said, "They're cute together, aren't they?"

"Who?"

"'Who'." I smacked his arm. "Annie and Rufus."

"And Moe. Don't forget Moe."

"You're not taking this seriously enough."

He shrugged in the dark. "They seem well-suited. They've known each other a long time and they still get along. Maybe it'll work out – or maybe it won't. Annie's been married before, but I don't know if Rufus has ever had a girlfriend, let alone a serious relationship." He paused. "At least she knows his capabilities and isn't afraid of them – that's huge, I think."

I got up on an elbow. "I didn't ask for your opinion about whether their relationship would go the distance. All I said was they were cute together."

"I know you, Raney. The rest of it was implied."

I lay back down again. Silence ensued for a moment. Then Collum asked, in sort of a strangled tone, "Do I make you happy?"

"Yes," I said at once. He let out a breath, and my heart turned over. Emboldened, I said, "Do I make *you* happy?"

"Always," he said.

"Well, then," I said, but inside I was singing.

Chapter 9 – Just your typical Monday

I was having such a nice dream when Rufus pounded on the door. I was drifting on a calm sea, diving deep for tiny shrimp, the sun warming my back under its shell when I surfaced. I had swum into a tropical cove and was just about to get friendly with another of my kind, and *bang bang bang!*

"Raney? Collum! For God's sake, open up!" *Bang bang bang bang BANG!*

"Keep your shirt on," Collum mumbled, rolling out of bed and pulling on a pair of shorts. He whipped open the door before Rufus could knock again. "What's the matter with you?" he hissed. "You'll wake the whole hotel! Do you *want* them to throw us out?"

"They might anyway," Rufus said, shoving a newspaper at him.

Collum took a look at the paper. Then he froze, the color draining from his face.

"What is it?" I said, reaching for my robe.

"Somebody got a picture of me in the caldera yesterday," Rufus said. He stepped all the way in but left the door open.

I vaulted over the bed and bounced to my feet, then took one side of the paper out of Collum's hand so I could see the photo for myself. Then I glanced at each of the guys in turn. "At least he got your good side."

"Right? You can hardly tell my shoes are smoking."

Collum slowly shook his head. "Please tell me this is a local paper."

"I wish I could," Rufus said. "But no. It's published in Hilo. Covers the whole island."

Gail appeared at our door, looking only slightly more put together than I felt. "What's the big deal?"

"Remember last night, when I said I might be the person to fuck everything up?" Rufus said.

She looked at him in alarm, then at the paper, then at him again. "I *told* you!"

"Yeah, you did," he admitted. "Could you please stop saying that?"

She snatched the paper away from us. "This is not good."

"Nope," I said. "Not even a little bit. If my father hadn't already figured out that he's been had, he knows now."

"We need to move," Gail said.

"And do what?" asked Rufus.

"Check out of the hotel!" she said, raising both her hands and her voice. "Get a B&B near the heiau! Something!"

"We could stay with Annie," he suggested hopefully.

"Sure," said Collum. "And drag her and Auntie Helen into this." He opened his suitcase on the bed and began throwing his clothes into it.

"Auntie Helen can take care of herself," Rufus said tentatively. He was quiet for a moment. "I'll go pack."

"Good idea," Gail said. "I'll check the internet for another place to stay."

Ten minutes later, Collum, Rufus, and I met in the hotel lobby. Rufus wore a "Union YES!" baseball cap, pulled low.

"Dude, you're not really disguised in that," Collum said. I saw his point. Damien knew what Rufus did for a living.

"It's all I had, man," Rufus said defensively.

"Let's get you something else," I said, towing Rufus to the gift shop. I'd just finished purchasing him a navy blue hat with King Kamehameha embroidered on the front when Gail came to find us. She nodded her surprised approval at Rufus's new headgear. "Very classy. Didn't know you had it in you."

"Ha," said Rufus. "You're hilarious." He stuffed his old hat in his duffel bag.

"We're all set," she said to me. "Come on."

Collum was already in the car. When he saw us walk outside, he started the engine and popped the trunk. We stowed our stuff, then got in. I was still buckling my seatbelt when we pulled onto Crater Rim Drive. "What's the hurry?" I said.

"I want to put some miles between us and the park before Damien has a chance to get down this way." He glanced in the rear view mirror. "Gail, you've got the map, right?"

She pulled out an actual paper map. Rufus nodded when he saw it. "Going old school. I like it."

"It's safer than using GPS on any of our phones," she said, "in case Damien has a way to track it." She pointed at locations on the map as she continued. "The way I figure it, it's going to take Damien about two hours to get from the Waipio Valley to Volcanoes National Park. He'll have to go to Hilo and take Route 11."

"Can't he cut across the island?" Rufus asked.

She said patiently, "There are volcanoes in the way."

He nodded. "Right. Good point."

She threw him an annoyed glance, which he pointedly missed. "Anyway," she said, "once he gets to the park, he'll have to chat up the rangers to find out where we've been staying, and then chat up the hotel clerk to try to find out where we're off to. Assuming he gets any sort of lead on us at all, he'll have to drive another hour to get where we're going." She folded up the map.

"How long before he gets here?" Collum asked. "Realistically speaking."

"Worst-case scenario? Assuming he read the paper with his morning coffee and got on the road not long after, and didn't hit any traffic on the way, I calculate he'll be arriving in Volcano Village very shortly."

I shuddered. "Heads up for golems."

But the fates – or the Hawaiian spirits – were with us. There was no sign of Damien or Surgat, or of any of their clay men, on our second drive to the southernmost tip of America. And the farther we got from Volcano Village, the easier I could breathe.

The place Gail had booked for us on the fly was very different from the hotel we'd just left. It was not a historic structure, for one thing. It was just a regular old motel with regular, cookie-cutter rooms. And the view, while lush and tropical, featured no smoking volcanic craters. A sigh escaped Rufus when he got to his room – it had a stellar view of Route 11 and that was about it. But he sucked it up and moved his stuff in.

Our room had a queen-size bed with a mattress that had seen better days. I sat on the edge and bounced a bit, then lay back and let out a groan of dismay.

"That bad?" Collum asked.

"Let's just say I hope we don't have to stay here too long."

The motel did have a pool, and we convened there with vending-machine snacks to plot our descent to Pele's Pit. "Let me get to the water," I said. "I can track down a sea turtle and…"

"Communicate with him?" Collum asked. "How?"

He had a point. The friendly turtle on Waikiki had communicated by poking me. "It'll be easier once I'm in the water," I said with more confidence than I felt.

"What if the turtle can't retrieve the Key?" asked Rufus.

"Can't or won't?" Collum said.

"Doesn't matter, does it? Either way, we're going to need someone or something fireproof to go down there with Raney. Something with a bigger brain than a sea turtle's."

"Meaning you," I said.

He raised his chin. "Yeah. Meaning me."

"How are you planning to avoid the bends?" Collum argued. "Raney becomes Water and Gail becomes Air. I've yet to see you become Fire in the same way. Can you?"

Rufus matched his stare. "No," he said at last. "But I think I know a way to get around it."

"Let's hear it," said Collum.

In response, Rufus doffed his hat. Underneath was Moe, the gecko who had befriended him at Kilauea.

"Hey, little dude!" I said, delighted. "Did you have a nice ride under the hat?"

"He's adorable," Gail said. "But he can't withstand Fire any better than I can."

"You'd be surprised. In fact, you're *going* to be surprised." Rufus bent over so Moe could jump down. The little guy ran through a gap in the fence around the pool and stopped at a spot several hundred feet away."

"It's so cool to watch them move," I said. And then I said, "Whoa." Because Moe was having a growth spurt. Right before our eyes, he expanded to the height of the fence. In another blink, he could reach the roof. Moreover, his neck lengthened, and so did his snout. Then he huffed experimentally a couple of times, opened his mouth, and breathed fire. Like, actual fire. A low-hanging fern leaf turned brown, curled up, and crumpled away.

"You taught him how to do that?" I asked, entranced.

"Of course not. He already knew. Remember when Annie said the Hawaiian word for lizard is the same as the word for dragon? This is why." Then his face fell. "Oh. I didn't get to say goodbye to Annie."

"We can stop in to see her once we have the Fire Key in hand," Collum said.

"Yeah. That's a good idea," Rufus said. "Anyway, Moe here tells me he's done some deep diving in dragon form and he doesn't get the bends. And clearly he can withstand fire. I think he's our solution."

"I want to go first, though," I said. "I can do the reconnaissance run, just so we know where Moe needs to go. Then I'll come up and reassemble, and Moe can go down."

The dragon's nostrils puffed smoke as he shook his head.

"He says he'll go down with you," Rufus said. "It'll save time."

I looked doubtfully between our Madman and the green, scaly dragon who was rapidly shrinking to gecko size again. "Um. How long can he sustain the dragon form? I'm not going to end up with a sick gecko down there, am I?"

"He can sustain it for as long as he needs to," Rufus said, looking to Moe for confirmation.

I sighed. "Well, okay. He's right that one dive will be faster than two. As long as he knows he won't be able to see me. I usually can't communicate with anything but Water spirits when I'm disassembled."

"He knows," Rufus said. "Plus he likes you."

"Swell," I said. "Raney Meadows, fan favorite of all magical creatures." I bent down and held my hand out for the gecko. He jumped onto my arm, then raced up to perch on my head.

That got a big laugh out of everybody. I raised my eyes in the general direction of my hair. "Do me a favor, will you, Moe? If you need to poop or pee, get down."

We got back into the car and headed for the closest town for lunch. Rufus drove and Collum, as the navigator, sat shotgun. That gave me plenty of time to scan for motionless clay figures in the vegetation on either side of the road.

I wasn't the only one with my father on her mind. "We can probably expect Damien to show up any time now," Gail said quietly.

"Fast food it is," Rufus said. "And then back to the heiau. Might as well get this over with, right?"

Twenty minutes later, a grease bomb sitting heavily in my belly, we hit the road again for South Point. I chewed on a fingernail as we drove past our hotel, but there was no sign there of anything untoward – no golems, no demon, and no Damien. So far things were going great, other than my nerves taking a beating.

I should have known it couldn't last.

Right where the paved road ended, we spotted our first golem in the grass.

"Sentry," Collum said, pointing him out.

"Shit," said Rufus, with feeling.

Gail lowered her window. "Be back soon," she said, and breezily disappeared. Her seat belt slumped as if it had deflated.

I unlatched it in preparation for her return. "By any chance," I asked Rufus as I worked, "have you explained to Moe about the golems?"

"Yeah. He says he's got it covered." He glanced at me in the rear-view mirror. "You okay?"

I shrugged. "Do I have a choice?"

We drove on. At about the point where the gravel road petered out, Gail blew back in. "Damien's not here yet," she said.

Collum turned around. "You didn't see him?"

"Nope. And the menehune confirmed it."

Rufus glanced back at her. "You called them?"

"No, they were already at the shrine. They knew we were coming somehow."

"How, though?" Collum asked. "*We* didn't even know we were coming until a few hours ago."

"The guardians must have found out somehow," Gail said.

"Whoever they are," I added.

Moe poked his head out of the hole in back of Rufus's ballcap. I could have sworn he winked at me.

I looked from him to my honu ring, and daylight dawned. "Wait a minute," I said. "The sea turtle, and" – I looked at Gail – "the hawk that led you here, and now Moe. They're all aumakua. Family gods. And they've all helped us." I looked around at my team. My adopted family. "They must be the guardians."

Moe jumped through the hole to Rufus's seat back. I reached out my hand and he clambered onto it. He let out a little cry and climbed up onto my head. Surprised laughter bubbled out of me.

"I bet you're right," Gail said.

Collum harrumphed. "I got a rock," he said dolefully.

Rufus grinned at him. "You may be saying that as a joke, but rocks can be aumakua, too. In fact, lots of things can be aumakua – sharks, octopi, dogs. Even caterpillars and clouds. And some plants, as well."

"Maybe yours isn't a rock," I said to Collum. "Maybe it's a plant."

"It's a rock," he said, sounding like Eeyore. "I'm sure of it."

I giggled. The situation was so absurd – here we were, driving to what might be our doom. I had a gecko on my head and my favorite gnome was going on about a rock.

Gail snapped me back to reality. "There's another golem up here on the left," she said. Sure enough, there it was, hunkered down in the grass a few yards from the road. We were silent as Rufus navigated us slowly past it.

"I'm going to get as close as I can to the heiau," Rufus said. "Any idea how far away Damien is?"

"The menehune didn't know," Gail said. "Only that he's coming."

"Any more golems?" Collum asked.

"I only saw those two."

That wasn't as comforting as she meant it to be.

We were nearly to the cliff's edge when I couldn't take it anymore. "Stop, Rufus," I said. "I need to get out." I unhooked my seat belt and had the door open before the car came to a full stop.

"Raney?" Collum asked as I skipped out the open door. I waved without looking at him. Something was driving me to the beach now now *now*.

I heard the others behind me, chattering their concern for me, remarking on the absence of fishermen along the cliff's edge and speculating that the menehune had told them to scram. I had no bandwidth for their concerns – only for the big Water pulling me toward it and the task ahead of me.

Moe jumped down as I crossed the dune between the heiau and the beach. There was no cliff here and the approach to the ocean was not nearly as steep a drop, but I could feel the currents swirling around the point that made this side a more treacherous put-in for canoes. Luckily, I was not a canoe.

Nor was Moe. As we made our way to the water, he'd begun morphing into his dragon shape.

And now I saw our welcoming committee: twenty or more menehune, in two lines like a gantlet. Some of them had drums, and they pounded out a rhythm that matched my footsteps and the beat of my heart. I nodded to each as I made my way to the water. Then in a swift motion, I pulled my sundress up over my head, kicked off my panties and sandals, and left them piled haphazardly near the surf. I had no time to neatly fold my clothing and leave it out of the reach of the tide. Inside my skull, my brain buzzed with need.

I'd been in the ocean countless times; it had never affected me this way before. Something else was going on. Something was pulling on me to get in and get going.

So I did.

Instantly, I was surrounded by a group of sea turtles. They cruised and cavorted around me, welcoming me to their home. Then they nudged me out to sea.

I looked around for Moe; he was swimming near me, staying clear of the turtles. For their part, they ignored him.

Satisfied, I let myself go to pieces. The current caught me and swept me toward Loihi.

The seamount is twenty-two miles from South Point, but we seemed to cover the distance in no time at all. A distant part of my mind wondered whether we'd gone through the Otherworld. Tiger made her own gates, after all – I presumed the honu could, as well.

It hardly mattered. As we approached the baby volcano, I figured it would be an easy caper – with no Damien in our way, all we needed to do was have the honu show us where they'd stashed the Fire Key. Then Moe would swim in and grab it and we would hightail it back to shore. Piece of cake.

Oh haha. When we were nearly on top of the volcano, I realized some of the things I'd thought were rocks weren't rocks at all. They were golems. A lot of golems. About twenty-five of them, positioned in a ring around Pele's Pit.

No wonder Damien was taking his sweet time getting here. All *he* had to do was wait on land while Surgat's golems forced us to retrieve the Key for them.

Chapter 10 – Monday, down where it's wetter

I sort of oozed to a halt and tried to force myself not to panic. I knew there must be a way out of this situation. I just couldn't think what it would be.

I'd gone up against two golems by myself in an Irish bog, but disabled only one. If the Irish god of blacksmiths hadn't come along in a timely fashion and done in the other one, undine half or no undine half, I'd be turning into a bog body right now. There was no way I could fight off twenty-five golems on my own.

And the honu were gone. I looked around, dismayed. Did they bail? Not that I could blame them – they had no natural defense against golems, either.

For that matter, where was Moe? He, at least, could slag them with his fiery breath – assuming the ocean wouldn't douse his flame.

There sure were a lot of things we hadn't thought through when we came up with this spur-of-the-moment, cockamamie plan. *Note to self: Don't let Rufus help with planning ever again.*

I was on the verge of giving up and drifting back to shore for backup– assuming I could beat my way back through the current – when I caught motion below me. I did a double-take, or as much of one as I could manage in my current state. If I'd been corporeal, I would have rubbed my eyes and looked a third time. The honu hadn't abandoned me, after all – they'd gone to get reinforcements. Motoring up from the deeps, tentacles flailing, hundreds of octopi were converging on Loihi.

Well, okay, maybe not hundreds. But there were a lot of them – too many for me to easily count. And they weren't alone. Diving in from above me came a flotilla of sharks.

The golems didn't stand a chance. As one, the octopi attacked, several of the huge creatures wrapping their tentacles tightly around each clay man and holding it still. Then the sharks moved in and bit through them, and the ocean finished them off by dousing the fire that animated them. The whole thing was over in less than five minutes, leaving piles of clay along the rim and drifting into the pit.

Where the clay met the lava pool in the pit, I heard – or rather, felt – popping sounds. It was as if the volcano was rejecting the alien clay from which Surgat had created the golems. As the popping increased, I felt the currents around me shifting, and I realized an earthquake was brewing.

I wasn't too worried about it. I knew Collum had the ability to stabilize the Earth's movements because he'd done it when we were in West Virginia. What concerned me was where Moe had gotten off to. And the honu still hadn't returned.

The sea was becoming increasingly agitated. I had a hard time keeping all of me together as I drifted around Loihi, looking for Moe. At last, I found him – snout-deep in a volcanic vent, digging with his front paws to widen it. I couldn't get too close – the steam rising from the vent was crazy hot, and I had a delirious notion that it could boil me away. And anyway, disassembled as I was, there was nothing I could do to help him.

In fact, I was beginning to wonder why I'd been so hot, pardon the pun, to come at all. Clearly the aumakua were perfectly capable of handling all of this on their own. Why did they need me to come? Because I was certain now it was the sea turtles who had issued that call that got my heart racing at the water's edge.

I mean, if it wasn't them, then who had it been?

Thunder rumbled and the current I was caught in became even more agitated. *Wait. Thunder?* How could I hear or feel thunder half a mile below the surface?

Finally, it dawned on me. It wasn't thunder, and it was only tangentially an earthquake. Loihi was getting ready to blow.

I drifted back toward Pele's Pit to confirm my thesis. Sure enough, a new cone was rising in the center of the caldera, and it was growing impossibly fast.

I made my way back to Moe as quickly as I could, and tried to find a way to get close to him without burning up. I needed to get his attention somehow. I needed to tell him to give up the search, that we needed to get to land, where he'd be safer. But it was no use – his whole snout was in the hole, claws scrabbling on the lava. And I couldn't touch him anyway – not without hands. The best I could do was sort of shove some water against him – which wouldn't be enough to get anybody's attention, considering the cross-currents caused by the earth's shaking.

There was nothing for me to do but leave him and hope he could find the Key before the volcano erupted.

Still, I dithered. Go now or wait? Risk injury from burns or the bends by turning corporeal long enough to drag Moe out of the hole, or repay his willingness to help by leaving him to certain death?

At the last minute, Moe backed out of the hole, triumphant. In his jaws was a box, smaller than a shoebox but bigger than a cereal box. Appropriately enough, it was made in the shape of a volcano. It even glowed red-gold.

If I'd been corporeal, I would have breathed a giant sigh of relief. *Let's get out of here!* I shot upward as fast as I could, as the violently competing currents tried to rend me molecule from molecule.

We were nearly to the surface when Loihi blew.

The concussive wave from the blast shoved us faster than either of us could have swum, magic or no. I surfaced and screamed, realizing as I did so that I had spontaneously reassembled. Moe was rapidly diminishing in size – I assumed fear hampered his concentration and kept him from maintaining his dragon form. Anyway, I grabbed the box from him, now that I had hands to hold it. He scampered up onto my head and I began to swim one-armed toward shore.

Scorching lava fell like rain, steaming away the water around us and quickly raising the temperature of the ocean to ... well, uncomfortable would be an understatement. Hot fog blurred my vision – I no longer knew which way I was heading. And it was only a matter of time before a chunk of airborne lava hit me – and then I'd be at the mercy of the boiling, churning waves, assuming anything was left of me. I had the Fire Key, but at what price? Was it worth the fight? Was it worth my life?

Lost in a rapidly-warming fog, I managed another stroke, and another. Then I gave up.

When I came to, I was lying on a green beach.

My first thought was that I'd passed through to the Otherworld, or that I was dead and green sand was a feature of whatever afterlife awaited Elementals. But if I'd been dead, I wouldn't have been dressed. And I wouldn't have been surrounded by Gail, Rufus, and Collum. I hoped. Because even if I was dead, I wanted them to have made it out alive.

"Collum," I sighed. "Why is the sand green?"

I could feel the relief that washed over all my friends. "It's olivate," said Rufus. "It's made naturally by certain volcanoes."

I pushed myself up onto my elbows, realizing as I did so that I was dressed again. "Which volcano? Loihi?"

"Nope," Collum said. "You're back on the Big Island. We pulled you and Moe from the water."

"How?"

He grinned. "Shortcut." Then his smile fell away. "I'm sorry. I held it together as long as I could."

I realized he was talking about the eruption. "You did great. You held it long enough for Moe to recover the Key. Oh!" I looked around in sudden panic. "Where's the Key? I didn't lose the box when I passed out, did I?"

"Nope," Gail said, holding it up.

I sighed and lay back down again, closing my eyes. "Thank God." My consciousness began to drift toward dreamland.

"Raney," said Rufus urgently, "can you walk? We need to get out of here before… Oh."

"Oh?" Collum asked. I heard him stand. "Oh."

So much for restorative sleep. I pushed myself upright and followed my teammates' gazes. There was my father, Damien Jones, standing on the cliff far above us – right next to a set of metal stairs. Gail was gone – I assumed she'd taken to the Air – and if Moe was still with us, he was hiding under Rufus's hat.

"There's no other way out, is there?" I said.

"Not unless you want to take another swim in a boiling sea," said Rufus.

"Thanks, but no," I said. "It wasn't any fun the first time." And anyway, even that avenue was closed to us – a line of golems marched out of the sea and filed along the length of the beach.

I got to my feet and walked toward the stairs. "Damien!" I called.

He laughed in Surgat's guttural voice. "Is that how you greet your father?"

I scoffed. "You mean my sperm donor?"

"It's not as if your mother allowed me to be anything else."

"Seems to me she made the right decision, considering you were holding her captive when I was conceived."

He tsked. "So much bitterness for one so young. Dearest Raney, your life could have been so different, if only you would have allowed me to be a true father to you. Why, you could have grown up in the lap of luxury. You could have had every advantage in life. But instead…"

The ground underfoot moved, knocking me sideways. I was used to aftershocks – I lived in California, after all – but this felt bigger than your typical aftershock, and it made me wonder what Loihi's instability would mean to the older volcanoes on the Big Island. "How about we have this conversation another time?" I called, straightening.

"Of course," he said. He'd never moved at all. "All I need is the Fire Key, and I'll be on my way."

"You make it sound so simple."

He shrugged. "It *is* simple. Although I would be pleased to make it harder." He turned as two other figures joined him near the stairs: Another golem soldier, and Annie Yamamoto. She looked scared out of her wits.

"If you've done anything to hurt her..." Rufus growled, stepping forward to join me.

Damien/Surgat laughed again. I could almost smell the brimstone on his breath. "Or what, little man? What will you and your lizard brain do to save her?"

Rufus's face turned red. I grabbed his arm. "He's baiting you," I said. "Don't fall for it." Louder, I called, "Are you all right, Annie?"

She nodded, eyes wide. I was tempted to ask her about Auntie Helen, but if Damien didn't know about her, I didn't want to tell him.

"Face it, Elementals," Damien sneered. "I have the upper hand. You are surrounded by my men. You cannot escape through this world – and if you try to escape through the Otherworld, well, I have your precious Annie."

"Let her go!" Rufus yelled, enraged.

"Give me the Key!" Damien yelled back.

The Earth rumbled again. I risked a look back at Collum. He stood as if rooted, all his concentration focused on keeping the Earth under our feet from shattering.

"Where's the Key?" I said quietly to Rufus.

"Gail has it." He concentrated on Annie.

"Where is she?"

That got his attention. He looked around wildly. "What'd she do with it?" he muttered. "Shit, Gail! Shit shit shit!"

The Earth shook again, and this time all of us fell. "I can't," Collum panted. "There's too much..."

The beach below us undulated. Then the green sand began to melt. "Rufus! We have to go!" I said.

"I'm not leaving without Annie!" He ran to the stairs and began to climb them.

Damien, at the top of the steps, laughed and laughed.

The ground shook again, and suddenly Annie screamed. It was as if someone had pushed her off the edge. "Annie!" Rufus cried.

"Gail!" I yelled, and ran toward the base of the cliff. I had half a mind to liquefy and break her fall, even though I couldn't have made a big enough puddle on my own. In the end, I didn't have to. Our Windy got under her and slowed her descent enough so that Annie landed on her knees.

Rufus ran to her and helped her up. She clung to him, sobbing.

"Collum, cut us a gate!" I yelled. "Come on, you guys!" We made a break for it as Damien screamed his rage above us.

Then he jumped. And, impossibly, stuck the three-point superhero landing – both fists and one knee.

I stood stock-still, staring, as my father slowly raised his head. His blood-red gaze bored into me. "Daughter," he intoned. "Come to me."

Unwillingly, I took a tentative step toward him. My mind was awhirl with conflicting desires. I wanted to flee. I *had* to flee. We had to get out of here – the extinct volcano under our feet was rising anew. But he was my father. Maybe my mother had been wrong about him. Maybe I should give him a chance…

I heard Collum call my name, but his voice seemed fuzzy and indistinct.

I took another step. Living in comfort sounded good. After all, I was unemployed…

My father stood and held out his hands to me. Collum called my name again, but his voice was faint and far away.

A third step. Nearly there…

94

Out of nowhere, an orange-striped cannonball sunk its claws into me, and we both went down. I wrestled with the cat, trying to get her to let go of me.

While I was doing that, I heard, rather than saw, a flock of birds — hawks and owls — descend on my father. When I finally looked over, he was cowering with his arms above his head, and he cried out as the birds worried him, pecking at his arms and his perfectly-coiffed hair.

"Thanks, I said to Tiger. "Let's go!"

"Where's the Key?" Collum said.

Gail materialized. "I buried it. Here it is!" she cried, pulling it from the sand. Then she cried out in pain, juggling the superheated box.

Something malevolent and sulfurous blew past us, snatching the box from midair.

"No!" I screamed, but it was no use. Surgat was gone, and he'd taken the Fire Key with him.

We were out of time. Collum cut the gate, and we all hustled through it — Rufus, Annie, Gail, Tiger, Moe, Collum, and me — leaving my father bereft and writhing on the hot green sand.

CHAPTER 11 – NOWHERE, DOING VERY LITTLE

The portal closed with a snap behind us as we collapsed.

We found ourselves on a beach very much like the one we'd just left, complete with green sand and metal stairs to the top of the cliff. The sea here was calm, however, and the beach was a regular beach – just green.

Out on the horizon, a mound of red and black poked up above the waves. A column of smoke rose from its peak.

Rufus and Annie still clung to one another. Collum sprawled next to me, staring at the sky. I took his hand and squeezed. He sighed and sat up. "I'm sorry," he said.

Gail huffed a bitter laugh. "What have *you* got to be sorry about? I'm the one who practically handed the Key to that demon."

"I couldn't keep the volcano from blowing," Collum went on, ignoring Gail's *mea culpa*. "It was too strong for me. There was too much magma to control." He let go of my hand and slumped back down. "I guess I'm not as strong as I thought I was."

"Neither am I," I said. "There were so many golems down below – I didn't even try killing any because I knew I couldn't kill all of them. And I couldn't get to Moe, and I couldn't get to the Key." I sighed. "I don't know why I even went down there to start with. The guardians didn't need my help at all."

"I should have told Moe to get out sooner," Rufus said quietly.

I stared at him. "You saw it all?"

"Yeah, I rode along with him in his head. That's some weird stuff, right there – being inside a gecko's head. Their thoughts are so *alien*. Sorry, buddy." He glanced at Moe, who was in the midst of a staring contest with Tiger.

"Tiger, leave the gecko alone," I said, as if it would do any good.

"But we were so close to the Key. So close!" Rufus went on. "And then we had it!"

"And then we didn't," rasped Gail.

"Gail," I said sharply. "You had no way to know when you put the box in the sand that it would get as hot as it did."

Her brow lowered. "I should have thought it through," she said. "I should have had a Plan B."

"We all should have had a Plan B," Collum said with a sigh. "Give it a rest, Gail. There's plenty of blame to go around."

"You guys just don't get it," she said, and was gone.

Annie blinked. "Will she be okay here like that?"

"Who knows?" Collum said.

I lay down beside him and draped my arm across his waist. "You okay?"

In answer, he got up and walked away.

"Collum?" I called.

"Just leave him," said Rufus. "He needs to kick himself for a while." He kissed Annie, then gently disengaged from her. "I could use some 'me' time myself. You gonna be okay?"

"Sure," she said. "Tiger will get me home."

He embraced her and kissed her again. Then he got up and doffed his cap. "Come on, little buddy," he said to Moe. The gecko ran up his outstretched arm and settled into the nest of his hair. Rufus replaced his cap and ran up the stairs.

Tiger blinked at me. *Are you coming?*

In response, I turned toward the ocean.

Fine. I'll be back to get you in a little while. When I turned back, Tiger and Annie were gone.

I sighed. For the first time in days, I was completely alone. For a moment, I savored the sun on my face and the sound of the waves lapping at the shore. Then I pulled off my sundress and panties, stacked them carefully above the tide line, and dove in.

This was not my Pacific Ocean, and yet it was. Mine was in the real world, if you will – the one where a brand-new volcano was violently cresting the waves, shaking the Earth to her foundations. This was a different ocean, where the Earth was stable and the air was clear. The beach here was still green sand. And the water was calm and inviting. It greeted me like an old friend and caressed me as a mother caresses her child.

It felt like home. And maybe it was. Undines all have their own home waters, and Mam had never told me where hers lay. Maybe this was it. Or maybe this was the primordial deep from whence all undines had sprung at the beginning of time.

It didn't matter, and so I let the thought go. My physical self had long since dissolved; now I released my worries and cares, my feelings of inadequacy and failure, and let the ocean do what Water always does for me: cleanses and purifies me. Makes me whole.

I drifted with the waves, this way and that, for quite some time. Some innate sense of self-preservation kept me away from the promontory – even here in this world, I felt, the cross-currents would be too treacherous.

When I surfaced, I discovered I had not drifted at all. There was the green sand. There were my clothes, right where I'd left them. The beach was as deserted as I'd left it – Tiger hadn't returned, and neither had any of my teammates.

I walked out of the water, fancying that I resembled that famous painting of the birth of Venus – except that there was no giant shell and I didn't have nearly enough hair. I donned my clothing, headed up the stairs, and began walking. I didn't know what else to do. Maybe I'd run into Rufus or Collum.

I wasn't worried about missing a connection with Tiger. That cat seemed to have a sixth sense when it came to tracking me down – not to mention saving me in the nick of time. I'd have to show her proper gratitude, the next time I saw her. I envisioned a trip to the store for albacore tuna was in my future. It was a special occasion, after all.

As I walked, musing about this and that, the ground suddenly rumbled underfoot. Startled, I glanced at the bubbling, steaming ocean, and then at the bilious sky. Somehow I'd managed to traverse the veil between worlds without realizing I'd done it.

Maybe our fight with Damien had shredded the veil. I hoped it could repair itself – I sure didn't know how to do it.

Either I'd walked farther than I thought, or stepping through the veil had sent me forward a few miles, because I was nearly to Kalalea Heiau. The place wore an abandoned air – no fishermen, no tourists, no menehune, and no other Elementals. Just a lone seated figure, dead ahead of me, legs dangling over the very edge of the precipice.

I stopped. I knew who he was. I recognized him by his perfectly-coiffed hair.

"It's all right, Raney," he called without turning around. "The demon has departed – for now."

Warily, I approached.

Despite the helmet of hair, he looked done in. His shoulders slumped, and exhaustion limned his face. Green sand had melted into the knees of his suit trousers.

I came closer, until I stood a little more than an arm's length away. "Why so glum? You're team's up three-to-zip," I said, bitterness etching my tone.

He glanced at me sidelong. "I deserved that."

Emboldened, I sat down. "You deserve far more, but that's a start."

He had no response. So we sat, not touching, and watched as the sun dipped toward the horizon.

"None of this was my idea," he said at last.

I bristled. "Capturing my mother wasn't your idea?"

"Actually, it was hers." Another sidelong look, this one with a wistful smile. "At least to start with." He sighed and kicked his feet. "I should have let her go."

Questions, acidic comments, and recriminations sprang to my lips, but I bit them back. More than scoring rhetorical points, I wanted to hear what he had to say.

Of course, he wanted to talk about himself.

"I suppose you've read my bio online." I had, of course. Several of them. "What it says is true, mostly. I grew up in a patrician family, with a mother who couldn't love anybody and a father whom I could never please. He died young, and I was grateful. It meant I could have his money without kissing his ass anymore." He glanced at me. "Sorry. I don't mean to be crude.

"Anyway, as I said, I took the money and built myself a business empire. It's easy to make a lot of money if you don't mind screwing people over. See, that's what keeps people from getting rich – they let their emotions get in the way. Thanks to my upbringing, my own emotions were dead. I suppose I should thank Lester and Sharyn for that." His lip curled. Then he leaned toward me a little. "Those were your grandparents, by the way. Lester and Sharyn Jones. Be glad you never met them."

I stayed silent, but inside I was hurting on his behalf. Damn him, he was getting to me.

"I'd never found them particularly trustworthy," he went on, "and so I never trusted anybody. Instead, I surrounded myself with things. Eventually, it dawned on me that I had a pretty nice collection of things. They were always the same, day in and day out. They never said one thing and did another. They never broke promises. They never made promises at all. So I built myself a wall of things, each one unique. But together they were solid, stable, and reliable. Dependable. They would never change.

"I convinced myself that my collection of things was enough – that I didn't need people, other than as servants and employees. I thought of them as disposable. At the first sign of disloyalty, they were gone.

100

"And then I met your mother, and for the first time I fell in love."

He turned to me. "It didn't matter that she didn't love me back. It didn't matter that she only wanted me for sex. I told myself it was better that way – no romantic entanglements, no messy emotions. But I couldn't let her leave. I had to *keep* her. Do you understand? I didn't know how to relate to another person. She had come into my life, and there she had to stay. So I had to separate her from the Water she loved, or else she would be able to escape."

"You nearly killed her," I said.

He nodded sadly. "I know. And then she did escape, and that nearly killed *me*."

"In a manner of speaking," I said.

He went on as if I hadn't said a word. "I'd let someone into my life and she had hurt me. She had betrayed my trust. She promised she'd never leave me and then she did."

"You lied to her, too," I said. "You told her if she left, she'd have nowhere to go. That her people wouldn't take her back."

"I had to," he said. "Don't you see? I had to convince her to stay."

I shook my head. "No. Lying to her was a dumb idea," I said.

"Well, I know that now." He stared out to sea again. "But it didn't matter that she'd betrayed me. I still wanted her back."

"You stalked her."

"I hired private investigators to find her."

"Damien," I said, "you *stalked* her. Call it whatever name you want, I guess, if all you're after is to feel better about yourself. But I *know* what you did. I was *there*."

"You were a child. You couldn't have understood."

"*I was there!*" I cried. My earlier sympathy for him evaporated as soon as he dismissed what I knew to be true. "Do you know how many times we had to move? Do you have any idea how many times I came home from school to find Mam packing? How many times we fled in the dead of night? How many friends I had to leave behind?"

101

"Friends," he scoffed. "They would have betrayed you anyway."

Retorts rushed to my lips. But I bit back my words. I wanted to hear how his story ended.

"Oh, but your mother was good at fleeing," he said with a bitter laugh. "I had to give up trying to track her by mundane means."

He was quiet for so long that at last, I couldn't stand it. "So you consorted with the demon," I prompted.

He turned to me, surprised. "I didn't call him myself, if that's what you're thinking." He turned away, but he wasn't staring out to sea any longer; the faraway look in his eyes was gone. "I simply asked around. Put the word out, if you will."

"How? Craigslist?"

"There are ways," he said mysteriously.

"And all you got were serious offers? No jokers?" I said. "Come on, now."

"I only needed one serious offer. And I got it." He looked away. "Boy, did I get it."

"Tell me."

The story was that a guy with a thick Italian accent responded to his request. He told Damien that he had called a demon into his service, that the demon had performed better than expected, and now the gentlemen had no further need of the creature. He offered the demon's services to Damien for free – no strings attached.

"And you believed him?" I said. "I thought you said you never trusted anybody."

"I don't. But I'd had no other legitimate offers, so I met with him."

The man came to the meeting carrying a green glass bottle that contained reddish smoke. The man, whose name was Domenico Buffon, said he was a dealer in antiquities, and that the bottle had come into his possession as part of an estate sale. In the same lot, he said, was a book that explained how to invoke a demon and make it subservient to your will. Disbelieving but still intrigued, he tried it – and lo and behold, the demon appeared. He then exerted his mastery over the creature and forced it into the bottle. Its name, he said, was Surgat.

"At this point, I was pretty sure the man was playing an elaborate prank. So I took the bottle from him and uncorked it. That's when I found out it was no prank – the demon was real. And moreover, Signor Buffon had no intention of simply giving him to me. Instead, he commanded the demon to…" He shuddered. "To enter me. And only then was the full plan revealed.

"Signor Buffon believes the world needs to be remade – and to this end, he is intent on unlocking a tool that would do the job. He called this particular demon because he had a reputation for opening any door."

"He Who Opens All Locks," I murmured.

His eyes narrowed. "Yes. Precisely. And since then I have been the demon's minion. Only occasionally have I been set free from his damnable control, and it's always when the thing has a new Key to deliver to his master." His expression changed to one of all innocence. "Finding you was never part of Signor Buffon's plan. You were never a target, never. I only wanted to find Ondine."

"But once I turned up, Surgat decided to capitalize on it," I said.

He didn't respond. Instead, he said, "You should go. The demon will return soon, and when that happens I will not be able to guarantee your safety." He took my hand, and I let him do it. "I wish we had met under other circumstances, Raney. I would never hurt you. Believe me."

His words lodged in the pit of my stomach and began to fester there. I wanted to believe him, but I did not dare.

I withdrew my hand. "See you around, Damien," I said, and walked away.

I had no desire to go back to the green sand beach – I had a feeling the green slag heap in this world would be the only one I could find now – and I definitely didn't want to be around for the return of Surgat. So I began to walk back to the car.

Partway there, I heard a familiar sound – as if someone nearby were sawing logs. I looked around and spied a pair of scuffed sneakers sticking out from under a bush. Suppressing a smile, I walked off the road and prodded one of the sneakers with my foot. "Hey, sleeping beauty," I said.

The noise sputtered and stopped. My favorite gnome poked his head out from the other side of the bush. "Raney," he said with a smile. Then, blinking, his smile faded. "We're back to our world, I see."

"Yup. Time to make like a banana and split." I took his hand and helped him up.

He brushed down his clothes. "What does that even mean, anyway?"

"I have no idea. Mam used to say it when…" *When we were closing the door to another apartment for the last time.* My father's promise drilled another hole in my gut.

I left the sentence unfinished. Instead, I said, "Come on. Let's get back to the car."

We found Rufus and Gail there, waiting for us. None of us talked about what we'd done during our time apart, but it seemed to have done everybody some good. The shadows around Gail's eyes had lifted, and Collum seemed almost back to his old self.

Rufus was quieter than usual, but he perked up considerably when we discovered Annie waiting for him at the motel.

Tiger, too, was there. *She didn't want to go home without saying goodbye.* Her tail swished disdainfully. *Humans.*

"Admit it, cat," I said, giving the spot between her ears a good skritching. "You didn't want to leave us without saying goodbye, either."

She didn't reply. Maybe she couldn't, as loudly as she was purring.

I glanced over at Collum, who looked deeply contented. "It's good to be home," he said.

CHAPTER 12 – THE LONGEST MONDAY IN THE HISTORY OF EVER, BUT THEN TUESDAY

Somebody – I forget who – got the bright idea to see if we could get pizza delivered. Lo and behold, we could. So we settled in poolside for the evening and discussed what we should do next.

I mean, the pizza wasn't fabulous. Then again, neither were our options.

"Next stop is Colorado, right?" I said. "I guess we should get online and book tickets. What's the closest airport to Mount Elbert?"

"Denver," said Gail. "We might be able to get a nonstop from Honolulu. I can check."

"You look a little green, Leprechaun," said Rufus. "Something wrong? Are you gonna finish your pizza?"

"*Yes,*" Collum said, scowling. "I'm just not looking forward to another long flight, okay?"

Rufus put up his hands in surrender. "Okay, man. You don't have to get huffy about it." He looked hopefully at Annie's plate. She picked it up and held it far away from him.

"Honestly," Gail said. "Just get another slice from the box. We got two extra-large pizzas."

"I just hate to see good food go to waste," Rufus said, helping himself.

"So back to the plans," I said. "We're flying into Denver, and then what?"

Gail shrugged. "The usual. Get a hotel, rent a car, head for wherever the Key is supposed to be stashed."

"How long is the drive?"

"About two hours, I think. Maybe a little longer."

"How long in the plane?" Collum asked.

Gail pulled out her phone. The search took longer than it should have – the motel wi-fi wasn't the speediest ever – but eventually she said, "There's only one nonstop, and it leaves Honolulu at 8:30 in the evening. Gets to Denver at about seven a.m."

"How. Long?" Collum repeated.

She looked at him for a moment, as if debating how to break the news to him. "About six and a half hours," she said finally.

"And first we have to fly back to Honolulu?"

She thought about that for a moment, then did a new search. "No, we don't," she said brightly. "There's a nonstop from Kona. We could make it tonight if we left right now."

Collum moaned quietly, picked up his slice of pizza, and put it back down again.

"I think that's a no," I said. "It's a no from me, too. We've been doing *so* much traveling. I mean, we arrived in Honolulu on Friday, and now it's Monday night. That's barely enough time to recover from jet lag. I'm not wild about rushing off again."

"I'm not, either," said Gail. "But there's one more Key out there, and we need to get to it before your father does."

"I don't think Damien's leaving tonight," I said.

Gail looked at me dubiously. "Care to share what you're basing that on?"

"Sure," I said, and told them about my conversation with my father earlier in the day. Well, part of it, anyway. They didn't need to know the family stuff.

Rufus sat back. "So he was waiting for Surgat to come back? That could have happened already. They could be at the airport right now." He glanced at Gail.

"Or they might have to drive back to Waipio Valley and get their luggage first," I argued. "Which means they won't leave 'til tomorrow."

"What if we all end up on the same flight?" Collum said. We all turned to look at him. "It appears to me that we have a fifty-fifty chance of that happening. I don't know about the rest of you, but I'm not crazy about the possibility."

"So what's your suggestion for avoiding it?" Rufus said.

In response, Collum looked pointedly at Tiger, who was snoozing on a chaise longue nearby.

I tapped my finger on my chin. "She could do it, couldn't she?"

"We'd beat Damien to Denver by at least six hours," he said, dangling the proposition like it was the grand prize.

"She would have to come with us," I warned.

"It's not like she wouldn't follow us anyway," said Collum.

Gail began tapping on her phone again. "You persuade the cat," she said. "I'll get the hotel." She paused briefly and smiled. "Guaranteed for late arrival."

Tiger was no dummy. I had to promise her albacore for a week before she would agree to take us.

Even instantaneous travel takes a bit of preparation, I discovered. I mean, you still have to pack. And then, too, saying goodbye takes some time – especially when you've just discovered the love of your life and now you have to leave her behind.

We gave Rufus and Annie some time alone. Nobody asked what they did with it.

At last, we were ready. We gathered next to the rental car, which Annie had offered to take back to Hilo for us. "I'll miss you guys," she said, hugging each of us in turn.

"Is Moe coming?" I asked Rufus.

He shook his head. "Nah. He's cold-blooded. He'd be miserable in Colorado."

"Aww, too bad," I said. I was going to miss my little dragon gecko buddy. Gecko dragon buddy. Whatever.

"Give Auntie Helen a hug for me," Gail said.

"I'll give her one from all of you," Annie said, and got into the car.

As she drove away, honking and waving, we turned to Tiger. "Okay," I said. "Let's go."

She didn't say a word – just walked forward and disappeared.

We exchanged a glance. "Did you know there was a gate there?" I asked Collum, who shrugged.

Tiger's head popped back into view. *Are you* coming? *Because if not, I'd rather go back to sleep.*

"We're coming," I said, and followed her.

The transition was a shock. It had been twilight on the Big Island and a pleasant seventy-ish degrees. One step and we plunged into full darkness, twenty-five degrees colder. I began to shiver. It had never occurred to me while we were packing to change out of my sundress. Now I was glad that I was wearing my ginormous backpack – at least my back was insulated.

"Ugh," Gail said as she stepped through at the back of the pack. "It's freezing."

"It'll be worse in the mountains," Collum said. "We'll have to gear up before we head out in the morning."

Gail bent to pet the cat. "Good job, Tiger – you brought us right to the hotel."

Of course I did. She submitted to the attention with more grace than I'd expected, given her rocky history with Gail. Tiger had some serious trust issues. At least she was speaking to everyone right now.

"Can we have this conversation inside?" Rufus said. "It's cold out here."

"What? Your interior furnace doesn't keep you warm?" Collum asked with a sly look. "I figured you'd be warm anywhere."

"Oh, I'm fine. But the Torrent's goosebumps are getting goosebumps." He pointed at my arms.

Collum wrapped an arm around my shoulders as best he could, given that the backpack was in the way. "Let's get you inside."

We checked in without incident – Gail had thoughtfully picked a hotel that allowed pets for an extra fee – and headed up to our rooms. The hotel she'd picked out was in downtown Denver near the train station. Our rooms were all on different floors, but nobody complained. Booking three rooms in a big city on short notice? I was thrilled we were all in the same hotel.

Collum and I took the second-floor room, which wasn't as comfy for him as a ground-floor room would have been, but there weren't any guest rooms on the first floor. I, on the other hand, could be happy anywhere, as long as there was a bathtub. Alas, this hotel didn't have any – instead it had one of those dumb modern shower stalls with a stationary half-wall made of glass.

"At least I got in a good soak this afternoon," I said, frowning at the arrangement from the bathroom doorway.

Collum kissed me as he brushed past. "Besides, we won't be here long."

"I suppose that's true," I said with a sigh, sliding the door closed so he could do what he needed to do in semi-privacy. "I'll tell you what, though – I'm glad I didn't dump my sweaters at your parents' house." I had considered it. I'd brought layers to suit just about any weather on my Appalachian Trail hike, the vast majority of which I knew I wouldn't need in Hawaii.

That hike seemed like a distant memory, although it had only been about a month before.

"You'll need a winter coat," Collum said. "We'll *all* need winter coats."

I plopped down on the bed. "And boots. And probably snowshoes or something."

He emerged from the bathroom and joined me. "We won't need any of that tonight, though," he said, pulling me toward him.

"I hope not. All the stores are closed by now." I snuggled against him. "Mmmm. You're nice and warm."

"Are you still cold? I can turn up the heat." He made a move away from me but I snatched him back.

"Don't you dare move off this bed."

Some time later, surrounded by pillows and blankets, we attempted to sleep. I should have been exhausted, given what we'd been through, but I couldn't do more than doze a little. You know how it is when you know you have to be up really early, so you sleep in fits and starts? It was that kind of night.

Collum, too, seemed to be rolling over more than usual. "What time is it?" I asked finally.

He raised his head to look at the alarm clock. "Nearly five a.m."

I groaned and sat up. "I give up. What time are we meeting the others for breakfast again?"

"Seven-thirty is what we agreed on." He flipped on the bedside lamp. "I guess we could take a shower."

"I have a better idea," I said. "Let's take a walk."

Collum, who was ever the boots-on-the-ground kind of guy, practically jumped out of bed to get dressed.

I pulled on jeans, a long-sleeved shirt, and a sweater, and hoped it would be enough. Together, we strolled through the deserted lobby – the free breakfast didn't start until six – and out the door.

It was hard to tell with the city lights surrounding us, but it looked as if the gloom of night was lessening. We followed our noses to Union Station – it was easy to spot with its big neon sign – and consulted a list of nearby attractions on a sign outside.

"Confluence Park?" I read. "What sort of confluence are they talking about?"

"Let's go see," he said, pulling me in the indicated direction. Which is how we learned that the park is on the spot where Cherry Creek splits off from the South Platte River. We meandered the paths and ramps, dodging early-morning runners, and eventually found ourselves at the river. The park's planners had thoughtfully provided a sandy beach, as well as a place to strip off our shoes and dangle our feet in the rushing water.

After about ten minutes, Collum pulled his feet out. "My toes are going numb," he said.

"You weenie," I said, laughing. He got up anyway and walked around, stopping now and then to brush off a sandy foot on the opposite shin. I went back to dabbling my feet in the river. The water *was* cold, but after he'd admitted defeat, I felt like I couldn't bail.

The sky was much brighter now. He got very quiet for a few minutes, and then said, in a hushed voice, "Raney."

"Hmm?"

"Look at that."

I glanced up. The Rockies were on fire – all pink and gold in the light of dawn.

I pulled my feet out at last and moved to his side. He put his arms around my shoulders without taking his eyes from the mountains.

"You look like you've just seen God," I said, teasing.

He glanced down and grinned self-consciously. "I kind of have." He looked up again. "As long as I've lived in America, I've never seen the Rockies in person. Pictures, yeah, but not the real thing." He slowly shook his head. "They are unbelievably beautiful."

"And we get to go up there today," I reminded him.

He squeezed me. "Life is good sometimes." Then he checked his phone for the time. "We should head back."

I looked regretfully at the river. But it was too urban for me to try taking a dip – there were too many people around, even at this early hour. I sighed inwardly and allowed Collum to lead me toward where we'd left our shoes. But as I finished putting mine on and stood, I glanced at the water again – and lo and behold, a face surfaced. The spirit of the river winked at me, then disappeared as the water rushed on. It almost felt like a promise. Like maybe four would be the charm.

CHAPTER 13 – TUESDAY, ON A ROCKY MOUNTAIN HIGH

We ran into Gail on the way back to the hotel – or more accurately, she ran into us. As we entered the breezeway in front of the entrance, it got especially breezy for a second, and then Gail was right there next to us.

Collum jumped. "I'm been meaning to tell you how creepy that trick is," he said. Gail gave him a wicked grin – all teeth.

"How's the air up there?" I asked.

Her smile faded. "Thin," she said. Now I could see little lines of worry in the middle of her forehead. She gave me no time to ask about them, though – she preceded us into the lobby and toward the breakfast spread.

Rufus, needless to say, was already there. "I wondered when you guys were going to show up," he said. By the looks of it, he'd already made a couple of trips to the buffet line. Gail rolled her eyes and picked up his used plates, then dumped them into a handy trash bin on her way to the food. Rufus watched her retreating back, then looked at us and nodded toward her. "Is she okay?"

"I'm sure we'll find out shortly," Collum said. "What's good up there?"

"Biscuits and sausage gravy," said Rufus. "The scrambled eggs were cold. I'd wait 'til they bring out another batch."

"Biscuits and what?" I asked.

"Sausage gravy. It's a Southern thing," said Collum.

"But we're not in the South."

He ignored that. "Come on," he said, placing a hand on the small of my back and propelling me toward the buffet.

I tried the biscuit thing. Maybe it grows on you, I don't know. The guys had several apiece. Gail seemed content with yogurt and coffee.

"So where did you guys hare off to this morning?" Rufus asked.

"Confluence Park," Collum told him. "It's a nice little spot near where Cherry Creek splits off from the river."

"We went wading," I said.

"Yeah, and I still can't feel my toes," said Collum. "We met Gail on our way back."

Her frown lines deepened before she spoke. "I went out for a flyover."

Rufus sighed and leaned back in his chair. "That's our Windy. Always working."

"It didn't start out to be work," she said. "It's a beautiful morning out there."

"It is," Collum said, and I nodded in agreement.

She smiled. "I love the mountains in the early morning. The air is so fresh… Well, not in Denver. They've made great strides here in cleaning up their air, but it's still a big city, with all the cars and industry and whatnot. So I tend to make wider circles – up into the foothills and out over the prairie." She looked past us, her gaze a hundred miles away from the hotel. "This morning was particularly fine."

"So what turned it into work?" Rufus asked.

Gail shifted in her chair. She sipped her coffee and put the cup down on the table before she replied. "I ran into some of the local Fair Folk."

"Wait," I said. "There are Fair Folk here?"

"Of course," she said. "They came here with the first settlers and figured out how to coexist with the local spirits. Which is more than you can say for the settlers and their relationships with the Native tribes that were here first." Her lip curled up at one corner. "But anyway. I spotted them up by the airport and we had a chat."

"Lookouts," Collum said immediately.

Gail nodded. "Watching for Damien. You might say they were surprised to see me."

"Because we're not supposed to be here yet," I said.

She confirmed my deduction with a nod. "They weren't terribly forthcoming with information – they've heard from the Irish branch of the family, I gathered, and they're all still sore at us for getting them in trouble with the Tuatha." When we were in Ireland, a fairy tried to sell me some information about our task, but I was too smart to play the game. Not long after that, some of them retaliated by trying to lure first me, then Rufus, into a bog.

I blew a raspberry. "If they'd dealt with us truly instead of playing tricks, the Tuatha would have left them alone."

"They'll get over themselves in time," Collum said.

"Maybe," Rufus muttered darkly.

Gail went on, "I did manage to get a little information out of them. First, Damien's not here yet – or if he is, he didn't come in through Denver International."

I considered that. "Is there another big airport nearby?"

"The closest is Colorado Springs, and there are no nonstops going there from Hawaii. No, he's flying, and he's flying into Denver. The only faster way is the way we came."

"Surgat can do it," I said, thinking of Damien sitting on the cliffside, bereft of his demon manager. "But he can't take my father with him."

"Yes. And I learned another thing." She leaned in. "The guardians of the Air Key are sylphs."

"Well!" I said. "That's a stroke of luck. We won't have to waste time asking around."

"It still may not be easy," said Gail. "I got the impression the guardians aren't all that crazy about the idea of giving up the Key to anybody. Even us."

We looked at one another. "I mean, I can kind of see why," I said. "We haven't had much luck with holding onto any of them."

114

Gail swished her coffee around in its paper cup.

"Maybe we'd be better off going up there and waiting," Rufus said. "We could just sit back and watch Damien duke it out with the sylphs for the Key."

"Now that's an idea," said Collum.

"We'll need to climb the mountain in any case," Gail said. She glanced at her phone for the time. "Let's find an outfitter and get the stuff we'll need for this jaunt."

Gail had done a stellar job in picking the hotel – not only did it allow pets, but there was an outfitter just a couple of blocks away. We trooped over there together just after breakfast – and after Gail extracted a promise from Tiger to behave herself while we were gone. "Even so," she said, "I put the Do Not Disturb sign on the doorknob, just in case. The last thing we need is to have to chase down that cat because a maid left the door open."

"I totally agree," I said.

As we walked into the store, I was instantly entranced by an adorable two-person tent set up at the door. "It's so cute!" I got down on my hands and knees and crawled in through the open door. "Isn't it cute, you guys?"

Rufus examined the tag. "It's no good for us. For starters, it's not big enough. There are four of us. And it's not a four-season tent."

"We could get two."

He chuckled indulgently. "But it's not four-season."

"Fine. Spoilsport," I grumbled, crawling back out. I knew he was right, but I still pouted. I made a mental note to come back later and get one for myself.

Collum grabbed a gear checklist from a stand at the front of the store. "Let's go look at coats," he said.

"Oh, all right." I tagged along behind the gang, goggling over all the shiny merchandise. Hiking the A.T. was cool and all, but the best part for me had been shopping for gear.

Rufus stopped at the cooking section. "We'll need a stove, won't we?" he asked.

"I've got one," I said.

He stepped back. "You brought it with you?"

"Yeah. It's back at the hotel. How do you think I was cooking my meals on the trail?" I stepped past him to the wall of freeze-dried meals. "We'll need to get a bunch of these, though. This one's not terrible. And that one's pretty good, actually." I turned to Rufus. "Are any of us allergic to shrimp?"

"Hey, guys. Need any help?" a sales assistant said. He was nearly as tall as Rufus and whip thin, with dirty-blond curls.

"Yeah, we're outfitting a trek," Rufus said.

"I found them. Rufus is looking at food. Guys! Coats!" Collum called.

"Right," I said. To our new advisor, I said, "What's your name?"

"Flip," he said with a grin.

"Nice to meet you, Flip. Come and help us out." I towed Rufus over to the clothing, with Flip following behind.

"So what are you guys planning?" he asked as I began perusing the rack of winter jackets.

"We need to climb a mountain," Rufus said.

"And when are you going?"

"As soon as we can," Collum said.

"Okay!" Flip laughed. "So you'll need several layers – an under layer to wick sweat away, then a shirt, then something for warmth, and a windbreaker on top. You might also want to get some rain gear – the weather turns on a dime at elevation, and afternoon storms are pretty common. Do you guys have backpacks?"

"I have one," I said, half listening while I kept looking at jackets. "This one's nice. It's, like, three coats in one."

"That's a good choice for now. If you were climbing a fourteener, though, I'd recommend something with more insulation."

"How tall is Mt. Elbert?" Gail asked conversationally.

"It's a fourteener," Collum confirmed.

Flip got quiet for a minute. "You're not planning to climb Mt. Elbert?"

"Yup," Rufus said.

"How soon?"

"Today, ideally." That was Collum.

"And you're just now buying your gear?"

"Well," I said, "we just got to town last night."

"From…?"

I looked at him. "Hawaii."

Flip shook his head and laughed in disbelief. "Oh, man. Look, you guys, climbing Mt. Elbert's pretty easy as fourteeners go, but you still need to work up to it. I'd recommend doing some conditioning hikes first, and maybe tackle a mountain that isn't so high. *Especially* if you've just come from sea level." His expression turned serious. "Altitude sickness is no joke. People have actually died from it. You should spend at least a week here in Denver, drinking lots of water and getting plenty of sleep, before you try to tackle any big hikes in the mountains."

Collum stepped away from the coat he'd been looking at and reached up to put a hand on Flip's shoulder. "Flip, my friend, you are absolutely right about altitude sickness. And ordinarily, I would agree with you, one hundred percent. But we just don't have that kind of time."

"We're on a mission to save the Earth," Rufus said solemnly.

Flip looked at each of us in turn – expecting somebody to crack a smile, I suppose, or start laughing. But nobody did.

Finally, he sighed. "Well, okay. It's your funeral, I guess." And then he started selling us stuff: Coats, hats, boots, crampons, day packs, ice axes, socks and sock liners, sleeping bags for everybody but me, a couple of four-season tents in case we got stuck out there overnight, fuel for my stove, dishes and eating utensils, water bottles, and lots of packets of freeze-dried food and snacks. I tried to steer everyone to the better food options and succeeded – mostly.

Flip also gave the gang a quick lesson in layering. While he lectured us on the merits of the various types of underwear – these are lightweight and super warm, those are engineered to wick away sweat – I spotted exactly what I'd been looking for. I picked up most of the stack and shoved it under the coats in one of our baskets.

Then came another lesson, this one in reading topological maps. I wasn't surprised when Gail told Flip she was familiar with them. They discussed the various ways up to the top of Mt. Elbert, with me chiming in, based on what I'd learned for my A.T. hike. I could tell Flip was still not on board with our plans, but he suggested the South Mt. Elbert Trail as the easiest ascent. "It starts at Lake View Campground above Twin Lakes. Here." He circled the spot on the map for us. "I'd recommend establishing a base camp there tonight and starting out first thing in the morning." *Assuming you're still planning to do this dumb, life-threatening thing* was left unsaid. "But check the weather forecast before you leave camp. September is usually decent, but you can get snow at elevation at any time."

"We'll keep that in mind," Rufus said.

Our new best friend led us to the checkout line and even did the honors himself. I slid over my card to pay for the whole thing. He glanced at the name on it and then looked at me, a wide grin splitting his face. "I *thought* you looked familiar," he said.

"Yup, that's me," I said. *Awesome. A fan.*

As he rung up our stuff, he said, "We get celebrities in here all the time. I waited on Kevin Costner a few weeks ago. And the Broncos players come by pretty often."

"Huh." *Okay, not a fan. A star collector.*

He went on talking. "I don't mind telling you that I think you got a raw deal. They should have let you finish out the season."

I blinked. *A Hollywood wanna-be?* "Thanks. I thought so, too."

He laughed. "I bet you did. I mean – I don't mean to be nosy, but what really happened there?"

I don't know what possessed me to tell him the truth. But I hooked a thumb at my companions and said ruefully, "I thought saving the Earth was more important than a stupid production schedule. The producer didn't agree."

He looked at our motley crew and said, "Oh." Then he went quiet.

But as he handed over our bags of gear, he had another attack of conscience. "Look," he said. "Please do yourselves a favor. If any of you starts to feel light-headed or dizzy or super tired, stop. Or if your heart is racing or you start throwing up, stop. Okay? And get to a lower elevation as soon as you can."

"We will," I said.

"I mean it," he said. "I'm worried about you guys."

"I promise I'll keep an eye on these idiots." I gave him my sunniest, most reassuring smile.

As we left the store, I heard another clerk ask Flip, "What was that all about?" A muted conversation ensued. "She is?" And then in dismay: "Holy shit!"

Still smiling, I turned and waved. Then I followed the gang out into the sunshine.

The temperature was beginning to pop up. "I just put this fleece on, and now I need to take it off," Collum groused.

"You'll get plenty of use out of it when we get to the mountain," I assured him.

Rufus hefted a bag over one shoulder and let it dangle down his back. "Was it just me, or did Flip seem overly concerned about our welfare?"

"Oh, he was right about altitude sickness," Gail said. "It's a real thing, and it can kill you."

"Although it usually doesn't," I put in quickly. No point in scaring anybody. "He's right about the treatment – keep an eye on yourself, and climb down if you start to feel woozy or sick."

"But are the effects the same on Elementals as on humans?" Rufus said.

119

"We're all half-human," I reminded him. "But honestly? I don't know. I know I didn't have any problems at Loihi. That's kind of the same thing, but in reverse – heavier water pressure instead of lighter air pressure."

"But you were dissolved the whole time," Collum said. "And Water is your thing. The only one of us who can get Airy is Gail."

"Not true," said Gail, looking at me.

"That's right. I can make myself into a cloud." I squinted, regarding Collum and Rufus. "I wonder what would happen if you guys tried to tap the Air essence you got from Gail in the energy transfer?"

The guys exchanged a look of surprise. "That literally never occurred to me," Rufus said.

"Dust," said Collum. "I'd be dust."

"Like a dust storm?" I asked.

"Something like that. I don't do a lot of shape-shifting, though. My Element doesn't seem to work that way for me."

"Maybe it would if you mixed in another Element," I said.

"Maybe," he said, but he didn't sound confident about it.

Rufus had been quiet through our discussion. At last, he shrugged. "I'm not sure it'll work for me. Air blows out Fire."

"Or blows it up," Gail said.

I had a sudden vision of campfire sparks going viral. "We don't need to start any forest fires," I said.

"Yeah, no. None of that," he said. "I'll keep thinking about it. Maybe an idea will come to me on the way."

When we got back to the hotel, the breakfast room was empty and the food was all cleared away. I heard Rufus sigh. To get his mind off his dismay for a minute, I said, "Hang on, you guys." I dug in the bag I was carrying, hauled out my special purchases, and handed them around.

"T-shirts?" Gail said, examining hers.

"*Superpower* t-shirts," I said, correcting her. The shirts were all dyed a steel blue, and they sported a cross between a mandala and a compass. Words ran around the exterior of the design: Courage, Humor,

Authenticity, Fun. "They only had them in men's sizes, so they'll be a little baggy on you and me."

She shrugged. "I'm okay with baggy in a t-shirt."

Collum clutched his shirt in one hand and gave me a bemused smile. "What?" I said.

"You got us a uniform."

Rufus winked at him. A smile dawned on Gail's face.

"Yes, I did," I said. "Now shut up and wear them."

CHAPTER 14 – AN EASY TUESDAY DRIVE (AS IF)

Renting a vehicle was as simple as everything else had been so far. Nobody questioned me when I paid extra for a big, badass SUV with four-wheel drive, even though the roads looked decent on the map all the way to the campground. The warning of the Fair Folk via Gail seemed to be on everyone's mind.

We loaded everything – including Tiger – into our new ride, and hit the road. I admit that I was pleased to see everyone wearing their new t-shirts.

"Quickest way is to take I-70 to the exit for State Road 91," Gail, riding shotgun, said.

"Any hairpin turns?" Collum asked from behind the wheel.

"I don't think so. Maybe one, but it's not for miles and miles."

We followed the directions from her phone's GPS, heading west on U.S. 6, the mountains looming in front of us until they nearly filled the horizon. As we approached the intersection with the interstate, though, the electronic signs for road conditions went into histrionics.

WARNING

AVALANCHE DANGER

TURN BACK NOW

"Avalanche danger?" I said, looking to Gail.

She shrugged. "It's possible, I suppose."

"Everyone else seems to be ignoring the warning," Rufus said, watching the drivers around us going merrily on their way.

"And 'Turn back now' seems like a weird way to put it," I said. "Do you suppose the guardians are trying to scare us away?"

Collum glanced at me in the rear-view mirror. "Maybe, but let's not take a chance. Is there another way to get there?"

"Yeah, but it drops way south. We'll lose almost an hour." Gail looked up at him.

Collum drummed his fingers on the steering wheel for a moment.

"You're in charge, boss," Rufus said.

Collum nodded. "I know. Let's do it."

"Okay. Take the exit for 470 right here."

The highway signs in this direction seemed calm enough. A few minutes later, we turned west again. Then we began to climb.

The sky, which had been bright blue and cloudless, began to darken. Thunderheads raced in from the west and north, blotting out the sun. "Maybe we should stop and have lunch," I said, eyeing the sky. "Wait out the storm."

"It'll cost us time," Rufus said, but he was gauging the clouds crowding in ahead of us, too.

Collum flipped on the turn signal and pulled into a gas station. "Let's get some snacks. Maybe the cashier will know what's going on with the weather. This storm wasn't in the forecast before we left."

As soon as we stopped, I opened the door and stepped out into a bright, sunshiny day.

"What the hell?" said Rufus. He too was out of the car. He ducked his head back in, then straightened, his face a mask of anger.

"Turn back now," Gail quoted.

Collum grunted and headed inside the convenience store. I shook my head and followed.

The cashier confirmed the weather report Collum had seen earlier in the day. "Where are you headed? Twin Lakes? It's a beautiful spot. Should be great weather – highs in the 70s." He grinned slyly. "Kinda wish I could bum a ride with you, but I won't have another day off 'til Friday."

"Too bad," Gail said. The rest of us stayed quiet, knowing the guy would be singing a different tune if he'd ridden this far with us.

Back in the SUV, the threatening clouds persisted. "Anybody know a way to counteract this?" Collum asked, flipping on the headlights. Big drops of rain began smacking into the windshield – or they appeared to be, anyway.

Gail hit the button for her window. Glorious sunshine poured into the car, along with a pleasant breeze.

As one, we all rolled down our windows. The illusion persisted out the windshield for a few more seconds, then abruptly vanished.

We breathed a collective sigh of relief and closed our windows.

Maybe fifteen minutes later, we rounded a curve and were confronted with the sight of a massive slide. It was as if the side of the mountain we were rounding just gave way, taking a tall spruce with it. The tree toppled with a loud *crack!* and dropped to the highway, just a few hundred yards in front of us.

Collum swerved toward the minimal shoulder and hit the brakes. The driver behind us honked loud and long, and passed us with a roar of speed. The three vehicles behind him did the same thing.

Collum's hands were shaking. "That was too real."

Rufus opened his door. "Take a break, me boyo. I'll drive for a while."

Collum nodded and they swapped places. I gripped my favorite gnome's hand tightly. He squeezed back. Then, to get the kinks out, he rolled his shoulders and dropped his head from side to side.

Next up was a virtual hailstorm that appeared, from our vantage point, to leave dents in the hood. Then high winds appeared to buffet us, threatening to blow us across the center line. Rufus fought to keep hold of the wheel, swearing the whole time. Yet whenever we pulled off the road or rolled down the windows, we were greeted by bright daylight. The only blessing was that through it all, Tiger slept on the floor at my feet.

By the time we got to Fairplay, the humans had had it. "This is taking forever," Rufus groused. "We might as well have stopped for lunch."

"There appear to be a number of restaurants here. Pick one," said Gail.

We parked in the shade next to a Chinese place and promised to bring back something for Tiger. She yawned, blinked, and went back to sleep.

The food was only okay, but we were grateful to be off the road. "How much longer 'til we get there?" Rufus asked.

Gail consulted her phone. "About an hour."

"Assuming no further manifestations."

"Right."

"And the chances of that are…"

"Slim to none," I chimed in. "Anybody have any idea what's causing this? I mean, is the car hexed or what?"

"And if we can't stop it, can we do something to mitigate the effects?" Gail said.

I looked hopefully at Collum. "Shortcut?"

He blew out a breath. "I thought of that. If I could figure out a way to get the rental car through the gate, I'd do it in a heartbeat."

"Cut a bigger gate?" Rufus suggested.

"You would think it would be that simple," said Collum. "But there would be ramifications – not the least of which would be introducing an internal-combustion engine into what amounts to an agrarian society."

I blinked. "There's a Prime Directive for the Otherworld?"

"What's a Prime Directive?" asked Gail.

"It's from *Star Trek*," Rufus said. "Basically, you can't use tech to increase the speed of development on other worlds."

"Not just tech," said Collum, "but yeah, that's the gist of it. Every world has the right to follow its own developmental timeline, without interference from more advanced civilizations."

"It's kind of patriarchal when you think about it," Rufus said, warming to the subject. "Here's Big Daddy Kirk, leaving these poor, backward people to wallow in their ignorance because we've decided it's good for them. What if the next stage of their development is *supposed* to be an injection of knowledge from a more advanced race? Societies don't always grow little by little – sometimes they make big leaps, especially when somebody figures out a game-changing improvement."

"But there's a flip side," Collum said. "It's too easy for a backwards race, as you said, to fall victim to a more advanced race."

"Slavery," said Rufus.

"That's one way to exploit people," Collum said. "There are lots of others. Take your average mine operator. He'd work his people to death if he got the chance. If it weren't for unions, the workers wouldn't have half the protections they have now."

"And even now, it's not great," Rufus said. "Mine operators hate those rules, and they hate dealing with the unions. They try anything and everything to get around them – regardless of whether it will kill someone."

"Exactly. The Federation weighed the pros and cons, and elected to err on the side of not exploiting any new civilizations they came across." Collum grinned. "And anyway, Big Daddy Kirk found ways around it multiple times."

"Not to mention the later series, which have been playing fast and loose with the idea since Gene Roddenberry died," Rufus said.

"Guys," Gail broke in. "I'm sure this is all fascinating to someone, but what does it have to do with taking the car into the Otherworld?"

Collum leaned forward. "It's a place where motorized vehicles have never been invented," he said. "They don't belong there. Horses, yes. Magic chariots pulled by cats, yes. Automobiles, no." He sat back. "Also, there are no gas stations."

"Well," said Gail, her lips quirking up at one corner, "if you'd told me that to start with…"

"Speaking of magical cats," I said, "let's order something for Tiger and get going."

The manager was more than happy to dice up some meat for our furry carnivore. They had no tuna, alas, but I figured shrimp would be the next best thing.

It was. *This is delicious,* she said, purring, as she devoured it. *I've changed my mind. I don't want albacore anymore. Now it's this stuff or nothing.*

"I'll make a note," I said drily. I watched her eat for a moment. Then I said, "Say, Tiger? Do you know anything about what's been going on in the car?"

It might have something to do with the fairy in the trunk.

I straightened in a hurry. "*What* fairy in the trunk?"

Collum had already hit the button on his key fob for the back hatch, and Gail whooshed over for a full inspection. "*You,*" she said sternly. "*Out.*"

Something whined in a tiny, piping voice.

"I don't care," said Gail.

More whining.

"All right, then – tell me. Who sent you?" She cocked an ear and listened carefully. I couldn't hear any more whining; I supposed the creature's voice had gone above my range of hearing. The guys were looking at each other, mystified. I guessed they hadn't heard a thing.

Gail's scowl deepened. Finally she said, "Just stop. It sounds to me as if you got yourself into it and it's not our job to help you out of it. Now you go back and tell…" Another pause, in which I heard the whining noise again. I guessed our hitchhiker wasn't eager to deliver any messages for us.

Gail finally put her foot down, metaphorically speaking. "What part of 'I don't care' did you not understand? We are *not* going to let you bully us so you can get yourself out of a jam. Now you go and tell the guardians we don't scare so easily." She brushed her hand around inside the back of the SUV, as if trying to chivvy an unwanted bug out of an open window – which, come to think of it, was basically what she was doing. "Get. Lost!" She scooped up the fairy with both hands and threw it up in the air, then slammed the hatch. I saw something sparkly zip around her head a couple of times. Finally the creature gave up and flew away west.

Gail dusted her palms and walked toward us. "What a pest," she said. "She's gone now."

"Who sent her?" Collum asked.

"Titania. Who else?"

"Titania?" I asked.

"Queen of the Fair Folk," Rufus said, his hand to one side of his mouth. "Try to keep up."

I punched him in the shoulder.

Collum said, "She's still mad at us for Ireland, huh?"

"Of course she is," said Gail, "and she's talked the guardians of the Air Key into opposing us."

"Super-dee-duper," I said morosely. "How long was our fair hitchhiker with us, anyway?"

"Since we picked up the car. Or maybe at the hotel when we loaded our stuff in the back. It was hard to tell." The corners of her mouth turned down in disgust. "She just kept nattering on about…"

We all caught that pause. "About?" Rufus prompted.

"Damien," she said finally. "She'd been on airport detail and screwed up somehow, and the queen sent her to track us instead. Told her it was her own fault that she'd miss all the action."

"She's a social climber?" said Rufus.

"Of course. All the members of the Court are."

"Wait," I said, my anxiety rising. "Screwed up how? How did she screw up?"

Gail clamped her lips shut.

"He's here," I said. "His plane landed and she missed it. You guys! We need to get on the road! Damien's gonna beat us to the Key!" I yanked open my door and sat in the back seat, trying not to hyperventilate. Here I'd been priding myself on keeping a tight rein on my emotions since Kalalea Heiau, and the first mention of my father being within a few hundred miles of me sent me off the deep end.

Tiger jumped over the seat and settled down next to me, her butt against my thigh. She curled up and began to purr. I skritched her under her chin and fondled her ears, and she purred louder. Tears trickled down my cheeks, but my breathing slowed.

Collum got in beside me. "You should put her on the floor," he said.

"Not a chance," I said.

He wiped a tear from my cheek. "Okay," he said gently. And as Gail started up the engine, he said, "We're not going to let him win, Raney."

"You bet your ass we're not," I said, and wiped my own eyes.

CHAPTER 15 – POSSIBLY THE LONGEST TWO-HOUR DRIVE IN HISTORY

You might have thought, as we did, that kicking our Good Neighbor out of the back of the SUV would have solved our problem.

Nope.

Gail handed her phone over to Rufus so he could keep us on track with her GPS. "One more mountain ridge to cross," he said. "Then we make a right onto U.S. 24."

"Roger," said Gail.

That sent Rufus off into gales of laughter. "Did you actually just say 'Roger'?"

She cut him a glance. "Yeah, I did. Would you rather drive?"

He threw up a hand. "Nope. I've had my turn. You're doing a fine job."

"Thanks."

About twenty minutes later, we hit a whiteout. The snow came out of nowhere – one minute blue skies, and the next, zero visibility.

By this point, rolling down a window was a reflex. Rufus hit the button, and snow – real, honest-to-goodness snowflakes – pelted him. "Come on, come on," he muttered, urging the window to close faster. When it finally made it, he turned to Gail. "Mamacita, we've got a problem."

"You're telling me," she said, kicking on the wipers and the defroster almost simultaneously.

Collum leaned forward. "Keep an eye on the big, orange poles along the side of the road," he said. "Just stay between them and we'll be fine."

"Right," she said grimly. "Assuming I can see the poles. I'm lucky to see the edges of the hood."

"Where did this come from?" I said, panic beginning to rise again.

"Let's just say I don't think it's a natural storm." Rufus checked Gail's phone. "And now we've lost the cell signal. Even if we wanted to try to find an alternate route, we couldn't."

"The map," Gail said.

It was one of those mostly useless maps the car rental agencies give out. Collum retrieved it from the seat pocket in front of him. "It's Denver metro only," he said.

Rufus twisted in his seat. "What about on the back?" He didn't wait for an answer – just yanked the map out of Collum's hands and flipped it over. Then he shook his head. "Nope, this is the only route. If there's another road over the mountains, it's not on here."

"Swell." The back end of the vehicle fishtailed as we rounded a curve, and Gail fought to keep the car from doing a donut in the middle of a two-lane highway. "Guess we'll just have to tough it out." She slowed the SUV to a crawl.

I started to tremble. "Are you sure there's no way to get the car into the Otherworld?"

Intent on the road ahead of us, Collum shook his head without looking at me.

I buried my hand in the fur covering Tiger's belly and shut my eyes.

We endured another twenty minutes of this unnatural storm. Then I felt the car beginning the descent, and opened my eyes. The sky was leaden, but the snow had stopped and the pavement was dry. I turned to look behind us; the storm was letting up there, too.

Gail let out an explosive sigh. "Is that Route 24 up at the light?"

Rufus scrambled to check the GPS. "Yes," he said, relieved.

"Good. Anything north of here, or should we take a break at the truck stop up ahead?"

"There's a town called Buena Vista a few miles up the road," he said, "but it doesn't look very big."

"I'll take my chances," Gail said, and turned right at the light.

We were now in a valley, with towering mountains on either side. To the east was the ridge we'd just come over, and to the west was a range of soaring, snowcapped peaks. In the middle was a valley, mostly flat, with a river running parallel to the highway on the right. "That's the Arkansas River," Rufus said.

"I've heard of that," I said, dredging up a memory from somewhere, although I couldn't have told you whether it was from the A.T. hike prep or from Mam, years ago. "I think there's good whitewater rafting and stuff."

That's when the wind hit us. It came howling out of the north, blowing so strongly that we had trouble making headway. We'd reached the outskirts of Buena Vista by then, and the wind was sending signs and garbage cans flying. A big can full of plastic bags flew out of the City Market parking lot and hit us head-on, bouncing on the hood and over the top of the car. I screamed like a weenie when it hit us. "Can we stop? Please?" I cried.

"Sure," said Gail, and pulled into a parking lot next to a diner.

As we got out of the car, the wind slammed the doors fully open. It was a chore to get them to shut again. We held onto one another to get to the restaurant entrance, and the door there nearly blew off in Collum's hand.

"Got a little weather out there," the cashier said when we finally got inside.

"You could say that," Collum said, panting.

She smiled. "Glad you folks could make it. Sit wherever you like."

We found a table for four in the middle room and Rufus passed the menus around. The wind howled like a banshee, making it hard for me to focus on food or drinks or anything, really.

In a few minutes, a waitress came by and got our orders. "Does the wind often blow like this here?" Collum asked.

"Not often," she said. "And not usually so early in the season. I'll get your drinks." She hustled away.

"I'd guess we can blame the guardians for this, too," I said.

Gail shrugged. "Wind is Air. Who else would it be?" She retrieved her phone from Rufus and looked at the map. Then she made a face. "Another half-hour to Twin Lakes, more or less. Probably more."

I groaned. The easy two-hour drive had already taken us nearly four. "We're going to have to camp tonight and start up the mountain in the morning, after all," I said. *Damien's going to beat us to the Key – again.* I didn't say it out loud, but I didn't need to – I could tell the others had the same thought.

"Let's eat fast and get back on the road," Collum said.

"Deal," said Rufus.

Nobody but Rufus ordered a full meal – the rest of us just got hot drinks and a snack. I guess the food was pretty good, but honestly I was just mechanically shoving sustenance into my mouth and trying not to freak out about the storm.

The waitress stopped by to check on our progress and did a double-take when she realized we were almost done. "You folks must have been hungry. Are you staying here in Buena Vista?" She pronounced it BYOO-na VIS-ta, like she'd never heard anyone say anything in Spanish ever.

"Just passing through," Gail said with a tight smile. "Could we get our check? We're in kind of a hurry."

"Coming right up," the waitress said, but I could tell what she really meant was, *If you're going back out in that windstorm, you're nuts.* I couldn't disagree.

Gail, Collum, and I stood by the door in varying states of anxiety while Rufus paid the tab. When he joined us, Gail tossed me the keys. "Your turn."

"Swell," I said with a gulp. But in a way, I was grateful. It would help my nerves to be piloting the vehicle. That might sound weird, but there's comfort in having some control over a situation – even if it's just the ability to stop the car whenever things get too wild.

We pushed open the door, grabbed onto one another, and did our imitation of a conga line to get back to the SUV. Collum moved up to ride shotgun; Rufus and Gail took the seats in back.

"This part is easy," Rufus said encouragingly. "Turn left out of the parking lot and head straight 'til you see the sign for Independence Pass."

"Okay. Which way do I turn then?"

"Left. But we have a ways to go before we get there."

"Okay," I repeated, and put the car in gear.

The wind had intensified, if anything, while we ate. Stoplights swayed like crazy above intersections. As we passed under one, the line holding it in place snapped with a shower of sparks. I held my breath and gunned the engine; I didn't breathe normally again until we were well clear of it.

The good news was that was the last stoplight – and as we got farther away from town, the wind seemed to die down and eventually sputter out. I eased us back up to the speed limit and began breathing more freely.

Then we began to climb out of the valley, and I tensed up again. What delightful trick would the local Air Elementals have in store for us next?

We drove in dread anticipation for fifteen or twenty minutes. Then, at last, the valley widened again – and I caught my breath. Ahead and to our left, massive mountains rose to touch the sky. Before them, a pair of lakes glinted in the afternoon sunlight.

"Turn here," Rufus said unnecessarily. "This is it."

No force on Earth could have made me drive past all this without stopping. At my earliest opportunity, I made a left off the two-lane highway and drove to the end of the blacktop and beyond. I *had* to get down to that Water.

"Uh, Raney?" Gail said. "I think if we go any farther, we need to pay the day-use fee."

"We won't stay long," I said, or meant to.

I have no memory of parking the car and getting out. All I remember is the muffled voices of my teammates, calling me back, as I stripped and dove in.

Man, that water was cold. The shock of it caused me to dissolve quicker than I might have otherwise.

All Water holds its history in every drop, but this Water was special. It remembered the last Ice Age.

As my essence mingled and danced with each droplet, I learned these lakes had once been glaciers. As the Earth warmed and the ice pulled away, some of the glacial water was left behind, like puddles after a rainstorm. Thousands of years later, men built a railroad through here, and people came to relax and play in these ancient waters, staying at a hotel across the way. Then the railroad went out of business and the hotel closed, and other men – important men – decided to make the lakes bigger. They built a dam, as well as a tunnel under the Continental Divide so that the lakes' water could be augmented by a river on the opposite side of Independence Pass. Now the Twin Lakes served as a reservoir – not just locally, but for hundreds of thousands of people who lived along Colorado's Front Range.

It was an amazing story, and I was glad to learn it. But I was more interested in information about the local spirits – in particular, the sylphs who guarded the Air Key.

The lakes did not show their faces to me, but their voices emanated from the depths, sonorous and slow, as befitted the ancient beings they were. "It is not a group of sylphs, but one. Her name is Anemone, and she has been here as long as we have. Only recently has she come into possession of the arcane device you call the Air Key, but she guards it fiercely."

No kidding. To think one sylph was enough to cause us all that misery on the drive here. If I'd been substantial, I would have shaken my head. "How recently has she gained the Key?" I asked.

"We cannot say. Not in human terms. Time moves differently for us."

That made sense. Humanity would be a flash in the pan for a being that remembered glaciers.

And it didn't matter anyway. "How may we contact her?"

The lakes boomed a laugh. "Have you not had enough contact with her already?"

"You raise a good point," I admitted.

"Hark, undine!" the lakes said suddenly, their voices quavering as if an earthquake were shaking them. "The sylph plans yet another attack on you and your companions. Go now and save us!"

Save us? There was no time to ask for further details. "I will," I said, and rose back toward the light, assembling as I went.

"There you are," Collum said in evident relief, holding a towel and helping me wrap up in it.

My teeth began to chatter. The air had turned chilly – almost as chilly as the lake water had been. "What's going on?" I said, trying not to stutter.

In response, he nodded over my shoulder.

Clouds were streaming down from the mountains to huddle over the lakes in a massive thunderhead. Slowly, the center of the clouds began to rotate.

"They're blowing up a tornado," Rufus said, joining us.

I corrected him. "Not a tornado. A waterspout."

Gail breezed past me and appeared next to Rufus, astonished. "I can't believe they think this will scare us. Waterspouts are nothing. Now, if we were in a boat on the lake…"

"Uh, Gail?" said Rufus. "It looks like the water level is dropping."

We all followed his gaze. "That's impossible," Gail muttered. "That's not how a waterspout works."

However a storm like this was supposed to work, this specific waterspout was reaching down from the cloud and sucking up a massive amount of water from the lakes. The spout's diameter was growing, too, as if to contain all the water. And ever so slowly, it was churning in our direction.

Collum put it together first. "They're going to try to drown us."

"It's not a they," I said. "It's one sylph. Her name is Anemone." I glanced at the astonished faces of my teammates. "What? The lakes told me."

Gail scowled at the broadening funnel. "Just one sylph, huh? That means she's outnumbered." She grinned fiercely. "Time to try out your extra added talents, boys. We're going to need to control that storm when it dumps on us, and channel it back where it came from.

"Got it," said Collum, and stepped away to begin building barriers and channels to the lake as fast as he could.

Rufus's grin matched Gail's for ferocity. "Water boils," was all he said. Then he stepped to the shore and yelled, "Come at me, bro! Come and get me!" As he spoke, he began to glow – first red, then yellow, then white hot.

"Raney."

Reluctantly, I pulled my eyes away from Rufus. My mind whirled with possibilities.

"I'm going to head up there and start untwisting the clouds," said Gail.

"Sounds implausible," I blurted.

"Maybe," she said. "But it's worth a try. And I have an idea for you."

"Whatever your idea is," I said, "mine's better." In a single, fluid movement, I threw off the towel and jumped back into the lake. Then all of my molecules sped to the spot just under the spout. A tiny jump and I was airborne, inside the eye of the storm.

I'd been right. The sylph was using the wall of wind as a reservoir. Hundreds of gallons of water were suspended by the rotating eyewall. Gail might have been able to unspin the cloud formation and Rufus could have easily breached the eyewall by boiling it away, but I was going right to the source.

I fought my way upward, bit by bit, until I was just under the magical floor that was holding the water in. Then I made myself into a happy little cloud and merged with the eyewall, just long enough to get above the level of the floor. Even insubstantial as I was, the spin around the eyewall made me want to throw up. I pulled myself out and waited until the dizziness subsided. Then I reassembled…and dove straight through the magical floor.

The sylph hadn't thought to overbuild the floor – she made it only as strong as it needed to be to hold back the water. My added weight, combined with the force of the blow, shredded it. Water gushed out in a torrent, back down into the lakes it had come from.

Mostly. The sylph had managed to get her pet waterspout close enough to shore to flood some of the adjacent property. But Rufus boiled a lot of it away, and Collum's impromptu channels took care of the rest. Together with Gail's efforts in the clouds above, the waterspout collapsed into nothingness in a matter of minutes.

I tumbled into the lake, forgetting to dissolve until the last second. As it was, the impact stung all along my back. I stayed in the water for a few moments, resting and pulling myself back together. Then, wearily, I swam back to shore.

My towel was right where I'd discarded it. I wrapped up in it as best I could, then joined the others and donned my clothes again with shaking fingers – as much from exhaustion as from the chilly air.

Gail breezed back to us, looking tired. "It's a lot harder to turn a cloud than I thought it would be," she said ruefully. "Thanks, guys."

Rufus, looking vaguely charred, nodded. "Sure thing. I'll tell you something, though – I'll never look at a tea kettle the same way again."

Collum finished smoothing out his channels and just generally putting the land back in the same state it had been in before. He, too, looked tired. Casting an eye at the western sky, he said, "We should probably find a campsite. It's going to start getting dark soon."

Gail nodded and began to head for the car. I started to follow her, but movement caught my eye. Far out on the lake, a figure stood: a beautiful, womanly figure with gossamer wings – wings she was alternately wringing out and attempting to unfurl as she traipsed across the surface of the lake toward us.

We stood still and watched her come. We were too tired to do anything else.

At last, her wings were dry enough that she could fly the last several yards. I was entranced – and envious. Dissolving was cool and all, but what I wouldn't have given for a pair of wings like hers.

Her disposition, however, left something to be desired. Fixing us with a murderous stare, she bellowed, "WHAT PART OF 'GO AWAY' DO YOU NOT UNDERSTAND?"

"The 'away' part?" Rufus said.

"I FIXED THE ROAD SIGNS, BUT YOU KEPT COMING. I THREW A BLIZZARD AT YOU, BUT YOU KEPT COMING. I TRIED TO BLOW YOU AWAY. I TRIED TO WASH YOU AWAY. BUT YOU JUST – WON'T – LEAVE – ME – ALONE!"

"Look," I said. "Anemone, isn't it?"

"QUIET, UNDINE!" she roared. "IT'S *YOUR* FAULT I'M IN THIS MESS!"

Now I was mad. "*My* fault? How is it *my* fault?"

"YOUR STUPID FATHER AND HIS STUPID DEMON AND THAT *KEY*, THAT'S HOW!"

"Here, now," said Collum, rallying to my defense. "You can hardly blame Raney for being born."

"She's really nice when you get to know her," Rufus chimed in. I shot him an incredulous look. In response, he shrugged. He had a point. I mean, there's not much you can say to an incensed Air Elemental that won't make her blow up further.

"Leave Raney out of this," Gail said, moving to stand between the angry sylph and the rest of us.

"AND *YOU*," Anemone went on. "A TRAITOR TO YOUR OWN KIND. THROWING IN WITH OTHER ELEMENTALS AND MAKING DOUBLE WORK FOR ME. I HAD TO KEEP BOTH YOU *AND* THAT CRAZY SOCIOPATH AWAY FROM THE KEY!"

"What in the world?" Gail said. "Anemone, calm down. We're here to *help* you."

"WELL, IT'S TOO LATE NOW, ISN'T IT?" she yelled. "HE'S *HERE.*"

As she spoke, a nearly-palpable scent of evil washed over me. I turned toward where we'd parked the rental car. Sure enough, a big, black SUV was slowing to a stop, blocking us in.

A moment more, and a familiar figure stepped out from the passenger side. "Well, well, well," said Damien Jones in Surgat's guttural tones. "Fancy meeting you here."

CHAPTER 16 – HOW TO CAGE YOUR DEMON

A whole bunch of emotions tumbled through me: anger, fear, dismay, disgust, and more that zipped through so fast I couldn't keep track.

Damien/Surgat watched me and laughed – a booming rasp that echoed off the mountains around us, making it twice as terrible to hear. "Dear daughter," he sneered. "Your feelings are written all over your face." His voice dropped into a gentler tone – gentler for a demon, I mean. "It does not have to be this way. There is still a chance to save your friends and be united at last with the father you have so longed for."

I swallowed hard. "How?"

The demon held out one of my father's hands. "Come to me."

One of my feet raised of its own volition.

"Raney, no," Collum said, pleading. "Raney!"

I paused, but not because of anything Collum had said. It was because I was watching my father's hand. Looking for something. A particular something.

And there it was: a slight trembling of the fingers. A fraction of an inch drop in the angle of his wrist.

I put my foot down. "Fight him, Damien!" I yelled. "Fight back! He can't hold onto you forever!"

The twitching of my father's fingers ceased suddenly, as if held fast in an iron grip. Then his skin turned dusky with blood, his facial features morphed, and at last we got a look at our true enemy – the demon Surgat.

Satyr's horns sprouted from my father's forehead. The nose lengthened and sharpened; the cheeks sunk inward. The eyes glowed crimson. The mouth – now a cavern full of cruelly pointed teeth – opened and mad laughter poured forth. "Oh, but I can," Surgat said. "I can

command any one of you. In fact, I could command all of you at once!"
Its voice dropped to a purr. "But today, I will settle for the undine."

Gail whooshed up to stand to my right. "Not today, demon," she
muttered. "Not today."

"Not any day," said Collum from my left side. Then he began to
solidify. His feet sank into the dirt and rooted there. I could feel his soles
becoming one with the bedrock.

"Um, Collum?" I said. "What are you doing?"

He took my hand and placed it in the crook of his arm. "Anchoring
you to the Earth," he said, in all seriousness. "Hang on." He began to
shake, and the ground began to move.

The tremor began under our feet and amplified as it shot out straight
toward our tormentor, so that we only bounced a little, but the demon
could barely keep its balance.

In my mind's eye, I saw again the demon standing firm at the top of
the stairs above the green sand beach, while the volcano under us roared
to life. "Oh," I said faintly. I got it now. This wasn't just about the guys
protecting Raney, even though she was capable of taking care of herself.
Nope, this was payback.

Collum and Rufus exchanged a nod. Then my magnificent gnome
held his hands in front of him, palms together, and slowly began to pull
them apart. The Earth juddered open, the edge of the precipice mere
inches from Surgat's feet.

Rufus raised his hands. Red-hot lava rose within the fissure, sending
plumes of fire into the sky. The stench was unbelievable, all sulfur and
brimstone.

Surgat laughed again. "Do you mean to frighten me? Poor, pathetic,
ignorant little beings! You have brought my home to me!" It bent joyously
over the fiery crack, arms spread wide as if preparing to swan dive into the
sea of flames.

"Hold that pose," said Gail. In a flash, she was behind Surgat, where she delivered a swift kick to its backside. The fissure's edge crumbled and the demon fell soundlessly into the pit.

Collum clapped his hands together. The crack sealed shut with a poof of dust. Then he flicked one hand sideways, and I heard a deep, resonant *ka-chonk*, as if a giant lock had slid home.

I was shocked. I had no love for Damien, but dumping him into a fiery pit seemed over the top. I was about to say something about it when Anemone squeaked. I'd forgotten she was there.

Gail clapped her hands together as if dusting them off. Then she strode over to the sylph. "You were saying?"

Anemone batted her eyes at us. "It seems I've misjudged you." She giggled nervously.

"Yes, you have," said Gail, her tone even. "But you can make it up to us."

"I can? How?"

Gail smiled. "Take us to the Air Key."

"Oh! Of course. Silly me! I knew that's what you were here for." The sylph was suddenly a simpering mess. "Well. You four just get back into that infernal contraption – I mean, your *car*," she amended hastily, "and I will lead you to it." She began to flutter away.

"How about this," Gail said, stopping Anemone in her tracks. "The three of them get into the car, and I go with you."

Anemone hunched her shoulders and glanced at each of us. She knew she'd been beaten. "Well, all right. If you'd rather."

"I would rather," Gail said firmly. To us, she said, "Go on. I'll make sure she doesn't play any more tricks on us."

By this time, Collum had unstickied his feet from the bedrock. The three of us made our way back to our rental car.

Rufus threw a glance over his shoulder at the lakes. "Maybe we should have paid the day use fee."

"Uh, guys?" I said.

"I'll drop the payment in the slot on the way out," said Collum.

"*Guys,*" I repeated. "What about my father?"

"Oh, he'll be fine," said Rufus.

"But you guys locked him in a volcanic rift," I argued.

"You heard Surgat," said Collum. "It's just like home to him. He'll shield Damien's body from harm because he still needs him to get to you."

I had to admit that made sense. "How are they going to get out, though?" I said. "You *locked them in.*"

Rufus said, "And the demon's name is…"

I side-eyed him. "Yeah, okay. I get it." I let out a breath. Damien would be fine. Probably. And we had stuff to do. I glanced at Collum. "How much time did you buy us?"

He grinned merrily. "I can't say for sure. But I made certain it was quite the maze down there. We should have plenty of time to retrieve the Air Key, and maybe even figure out where Surgat's been stashing the other Keys." We paused at the driver's side door. "It's gonna be okay, Raney. You'll see." He hugged me and got in the passenger's seat.

"Piece of cake!" Rufus crowed and piled in back.

I fired up the engine and pulled off the road to get around Damien's big, black SUV. I figured a little off-roading was the least of the damage we'd done here today.

Still, as we headed back to the highway, I found I couldn't be as cheerful as the guys were. We were still 0-for-3, we didn't have the Air Key yet, and I didn't trust Anemone as far as I could throw her. Too many things could still go wrong – and too much was still at stake.

AUTHOR'S NOTE

Raney's right about one thing – for world travelers, time zones suck. My daughter Amy visited Australia when she was in middle school. The flight takes about twenty hours and crosses the International Date Line, which turns time back a whole day. When she got home, she insisted on staying up past midnight to make sure the date actually moved forward.

In doing research for this book, I was sad to learn the Thurston lava tubes in Hawaii Volcanoes National Park were damaged by Kilauea's eruption last year. I enjoyed hiking in those tubes when I visited the park in 2010. I didn't know about Kalalea Heiau back then, or I would have definitely checked it out. Not only is it the southernmost point in the United States, but I've read that if you sailed straight south from South Point, the next land you would hit is Antarctica.

Twin Lakes is a beautiful spot and one of my favorite places in Colorado, so of course I had to work it into a book. I've done a little (*very* little) hiking, but the only fourteener I've bagged is Mt. Evans, and only because you can drive up it. Even then, I was tired and a little woozy when I got to the peak, and skipped the final 500 yard hike to the very top. Altitude sickness really is no joke.

I am not joking when I say that I'm eternally grateful to my editor, Susan Strayer, who has read all of my books and still keeps coming back for more. You should be grateful to her, too – I was all set to end this book on a horrible cliffhanger until she talked me out of it.

I hope you're enjoying the *Elemental Keys* series, and I'm grateful to all of my readers who have gotten this far. Would you do me a favor, please, and leave a review? I'd appreciate it – and so will the readers you'll be helping to decide whether to give my books a try. Thanks in advance! And be sure to look for Book 4, *Beach Magic,* early next month.

If you'd like a free copy of another of my novels, please go to http://eepurl.com/xxw9d to sign up for my email list. It's the best way to find out when my next book will be released, as that's the only time I send a newsletter. I promise not to overwhelm your inbox. Plus, hey – free novel!

Lynne Cantwell
March 2020

About the Author

Lynne Cantwell writes mostly urban fantasy and paranormal romance, with a dash of magic realism when she's feeling more serious. She is also a contributing author for Indies Unlimited. In a previous life, she was a broadcast journalist who worked at Mutual/NBC Radio News, CNN, and a bunch of other places you have probably never heard of. She has a master's degree in fiction writing from Johns Hopkins University. Currently, she lives near Washington, D.C.

Discover other titles by Lynne Cantwell:

The Elemental Keys
River Magic (original title: Rivers Run)
Bog Magic (original title: Treacherous Ground)
Gecko Magic (original title: Molten Trail)
Beach Magic

The Pipe Woman Chronicles Universe
Seized: Book One of the Pipe Woman Chronicles
Fissured: Book Two of the Pipe Woman Chronicles
Tapped: Book Three of the Pipe Woman Chronicles
Gravid: Book Four of the Pipe Woman Chronicles
Annealed: Book Five of the Pipe Woman Chronicles
The Pipe Woman Chronicles Omnibus

Where Were You When: A Land, Sea, Sky Anthology
Crosswind: Land, Sea, Sky Book 1
Undertow: Land, Sea, Sky Book 2
Scorched Earth: Land, Sea, Sky Book 3
The Land Sea Sky Trilogy

Dragon's Web: Book One of the Pipe Woman's Legacy
Firebird's Snare: Book Two of the Pipe Woman's Legacy
Spider's Lifeline: Book Three of the Pipe Woman's Legacy
Turtle's Weir: Book Four of the Pipe Woman's Legacy

A Billion Gods and Goddesses: The Mythology Behind *The Pipe Woman Chronicles*

The Transcendence Trilogy
Maggie in the Dark: Transcendence Book 1
Maggie on the Cusp: Transcendence Book 2
Maggie at Moonrise: Transcendence Book 3

Stand-Alone Novels
SwanSong
Seasons of the Fool

Short Story Collections
Back Home Again: The Five59 Stories, plus a few

Find Lynne on Teh Intarwebz:

Facebook: http://www.facebook.com/pages/Lynne-Cantwell
Twitter: http://twitter.com/lynnecantwell
Goodreads:
http://www.goodreads.com/author/show/696603.Lynne_Cantwell
Pinterest: http://pinterest.com/lynnecantwell
Ravelry: https://www.ravelry.com/people/lynnecm
Blog: http://www.hearth-myth.com

Turn the Page for an Excerpt from
BEACH MAGIC: The Elemental Keys Book 4!

I avoid watching or reading about the news – I'm always worried I'll accidentally see a photo of me that some paparazzi shot from a bad angle or when I wasn't wearing makeup or something. My reputation in Hollywood was bad enough – especially now that the producers of *Story of a Homicide* had bounced me from the show for taking up with this bunch of characters when I was supposed to be hiking the Appalachian Trail.

But I couldn't afford to dwell on my career, or what was left of it, right now. *Eyes on the prize, Raney!*

"Eyes on the road" would have been more helpful. Anemone breezed up a gravel road off the main drag – and when I say *up*, I do mean *up*. I gunned the engine and followed her, the SUV bouncing from rut to pothole.

"The rental agreement didn't prohibit off-roading, did it??" Rufus asked from the back. "Or driving on unpaved roads?"

Collum waved toward the cargo holder between his seat and mine. "The contract's right here, if you want to read it."

"Thanks, but no. Hey, Raney? You'll get more power if you downshift," Rufus said.

I glared at his reflection in the rear-view mirror. "Do you want to do this?"

"Well, actually…"

It was Collum's turn to glare at Rufus. "No," he said. "We don't have time to stop and switch drivers. Raney's doing a fine job. Leave her alone."

"Yeah, leave me alone," I echoed as I swerved to avoid another pothole.

Anemone dodged to the left, in the direction of a "campground this way" sign. Gail made a wide turn to follow her. "They're…"Collum began.

"Thanks," I ground out, and made the turn.

There was no campground host on duty – just a pay station with envelopes and a sign with the campground rules and costs. I took the first available parking spot near the bathrooms. "Okay, everybody out for a potty stop," I said as I opened the door and jumped down.

Rufus laughed. "Did you just say 'potty stop'?"

"Yes, I did," I said with mock severity. "And the last one out of the bathroom gets to pay for camping." I jogged across the dirt road to the ladies' room.

When I came out, Collum was perusing the map at the pay station. "Did you lose a coin toss?" I asked, sliding my arms around his waist.

He kissed the top of my head. Then he pointed to a spot on the map. "Here we are," he said, "and here's the lower trailhead." His finger moved. Then it moved again. "And here's the upper trailhead. If we start at the lower trailhead, it'll be an eleven-mile-plus hike, round trip. But if we start up here, it'll be only a seven-and-a-half-mile round trip."

"I'm all about the shorter hike," I said as Rufus joined us. "What's the drawback?"

"The road's a little rough to get there." He pointed to a photo that showed mostly boulders.

My eyes widened. "That's a road?"

"Claims to be."

Rufus was vibrating in excitement. "Piece of cake," he said. "I can do it, easy. The car has four-wheel drive, right?"

"I believe so," said Collum.

"I know it does," Rufus said, plowing on. "I saw the switch when it was my turn to drive."

I handed the keys over to him and scanned the parking lot. "Where's Gail? I said. "For that matter, where's Anemone?"

My first question was answered immediately. A breeze whooshed past me and settled into Gail's form. "Gear up," she said shortly. "She's not waiting for us."

"We're leaving *now*?" I said as we walked back to the car. "Isn't it more dangerous to start up in the afternoon? I mean, Flip said…" Flip was the guy who helped us buy all our gear at the outfitter's in Denver. He was very clear on the way big mountains make their own weather. The later in

151

the day it was, the bigger the risk we ran of running into a blizzard before we got to the top.

"We can't wait. Here." Gail handed me a hydration daypack from the back of the SUV.

I put it on, chattering nervously all the while. "But I thought we'd set up the tents and…"

Gail looked as if she were ready to blow. "And what? Take a nap?" She threw a hydration pack at Rufus, who caught it. "What do you think I've been doing for the last ten minutes? Having a lovely cup of tea with Anemone while we caught up on old times?" She grabbed two more packs, shoved one into Collum's arms and put the other one on. "That bitch is in charge, and she knows we're here to take the Key. She's not planning on making this easy for us."

"Fine," Rufus said, and headed for the driver's door. "We're not planning on playing her game, either. Get in. We're driving to the upper trailhead." He got in the car and grunted in frustration. "My God, Raney, do you *have* to pull the seat so far forward?"

"I do if I want to reach the pedals," I retorted, and got in back. Collum took the front passenger seat again. Gail, still fuming, disappeared in Anemone's direction.

The so-called road to the upper trailhead did not disappoint. It was exactly like the photo at the campground pay station in that it consisted mostly of boulders. I was glad Rufus was driving – if I'd been behind the wheel, I was sure we'd have broken an axle or something.

At last we arrived at the parking lot for the upper trailhead and piled out. Of course there was no sign of Anemone. "Well," Collum growled, "where is she?"

Gail popped in next to me. "Already on the trail and moving fast," she said, and popped out again. I fancied I could still see her glare hanging in the air like a Cheshire cat's smile. Except not. Well, you know.

"I'll go first," Rufus said. "My stride is the longest of the three of us. I'll try to keep sight of everyone," he called over his shoulder.

"Guess that leaves you and me," I said to Collum.

We shared a long look and a quick kiss. "Come on," he said.

That was the last thing any of us said for quite a while. The trail rose steeply to the northwest, robbing us both of breath.

I may be emotional but I'm not stupid; I had actually trained for hiking the Appalachian Trail. But the highest point on the A.T. is Clingman's Dome in Tennessee at 6,643 feet – lower than the elevation we were starting at here by a good four thousand feet. Also, we'd all spent a lot of time at sea level over the past few weeks. The air was a lot thinner here. In short, none of us were in shape for this, and certainly not at this pace.

Flip had tried to warn us. I should have listened better to him. We all should have listened better to him.

After an hour or so of manfully struggling upward, Collum stopped and bent over, gasping. "Just catching my breath," he said between wheezes.

"Hydrate," I ordered, and obediently he sucked from the hose coming from his pack. I did the same. Then I slipped off the daypack and pulled out a couple of Clif bars, handing one to him. He unwrapped it and took two bites. Then he shoved it in his pocket and started up the trail again.

I followed, silently vowing to stay behind him in case he keeled over. I wasn't sure what I could do if it happened – if he tumbled onto me, I wouldn't have had the strength to get him off me. Although I guessed I could force-dissolve and get out from under him that way. Assuming I had the strength myself to do it at that point. I decided adrenaline would be my friend.

Given my thoughts at that moment, I might have been a little light-headed myself. Luckily the elevation gain slowed as we entered an aspen grove. The switchbacks here made the hike even longer, but the golden aspens against the clear, blue sky made the process tolerable. Best of all, we finally had glimpses of Rufus among the trees, and he didn't appear to be that far ahead of us.

Then the trail leveled off and the view opened up. Aspens gave way to a mountain meadow dotted with conifers, and now we had an unobstructed view of Rufus some distance ahead. He stopped and waved to us, then pointed up to where our personal trail marker Gail was phasing in and out as she shadowed Anemone. The altitude didn't seem to affect the sylphs at all. I kind of hated them both right then.

Far ahead of them was the summit of Mt. Elbert – treeless and rocky. Something moved there.

I turned to Collum in alarm. "Did you see that?" And then, seeing him, I was really alarmed. "Collum, are you okay?"

"Just a little light-headed," he said, panting. "I'll be fine."

Yeah, he'd be fine once we got back to the campground. But first, we had to reach the summit, and we still had about three-thousand feet of elevation to gain before we got there.

"Honey, you're coming down with altitude sickness," I said, trying not to panic – or at least trying not to let my panic reach my voice. "You should go back to the car."

He shut his eyes and stood stock-still.

"Collum? What's happening?" I asked, and now I couldn't help it – my fear made my voice shake. "Are you okay? Collum, talk to me!"

He was silent for another moment. I had a quick mental picture of him becoming the mountain, or maybe becoming part of the mountain. As if he were adapting to its environment. As if it had always been his home.

He breathed deeply once, twice, and opened his eyes. "I'm fine," he repeated. He reached into his pocket and finished off the Clif bar in two bites. "Let's go." And he strode away.

I caught up to him. "Did you just cure yourself? You did, didn't you?"

He shrugged. "Mountains are Earth. I just had to tune into this one."

I clutched his arm happily, and he smiled at me. "Did you call me honey just then?" he asked.

"Did I?" I said, with a toss of my head.

154

He grinned wider.

And then I remembered what I'd been about to say. "Collum, I think there's something waiting…"

I never got the chance to finish. A sudden, howling wind took my breath away. The temperature dropped twenty degrees as clouds crowded out the sun. We'd been told to watch for sudden changes in the weather, but I was pretty sure they weren't usually *this* sudden.

I looked ahead for Gail, but she had vanished. So had Anemone. I hoped Gail had gone after her to make her stop messing with the weather, but there was no way to know for sure.

We struggled against the wind to reach Rufus. We were above the treeline now — there was nowhere to escape the ferocious wind and the bits of ice it drove at us. Our faces stinging, all we could do was plod on.

Look for
Beach Magic:
The Elemental Keys Book 4
Thursday, April 9, 2020!

www.ingramcontent.com/pod-product-compliance
Lightning Source LLC
Chambersburg PA
CBHW071918220626
47052CB00002B/409